TAKE ME HOME

A.D. ELLIS

Thanks to Blake Allwood for
*"**He picked my freakin' zucchini.**"*

ONE

MARCUS KINGSLEY

THE PLACE WAS A TOTAL DIVE, but I figured I was better off there than in my new—*very* temporary—town of residence. The problem with your family owning a tiny country town named after them was the total lack of anonymity.

Not that anyone in Kingsley actually knew me. But they would soon enough. Hell, Gran was probably at the local bar, Darts, Balls, and Beer—classy *and* creative—at that very moment telling her crew all about me coming to stay. How that woman ever made it in the city with Gramps was beyond me; she was a country girl through-and-through.

Coming to Kingsley was *not* my idea, and I was having a bit of trouble coming to terms with my new habitat. So, I'd given Gran a hug, tossed my luggage into my new room at the Kingsley Bed and Breakfast, and told her I needed to get some air.

I'd driven forty-five minutes away to a slightly—*very* slightly—bigger and better establishment. My hopes of an anonymous quickie had dimmed a fraction when I walked in, but I wasn't one to give up without a fight. The large circle of social acquaintances I had back in the city—I didn't actually have many *friends* other than my sister, Marissa, and maybe a couple people I was friendly with at work—knew that once I set my mind to finding a man to warm my bed, I wouldn't be going home alone. Totally metaphorically, of course. I never took a hookup *home* with me. That's what luxurious hotel rooms were for.

I sipped my extremely domestic beer and mourned the fact that no one within a fifty-mile radius seemed to know the blessed glory of an import. Glancing around the bar, I recognized that the usual twinks who flocked to me in the city were noticeably missing from the night's crowd of locals. Not all that surprising; in a Midwestern small town, I didn't expect to find a lot of open acceptance for flashy, beautiful twinks.

Even the aloof, slick closet cases who always seemed to find me an intriguing challenge were absent from the crowd. Again, not surprising. The neighboring town of Shilesville where I'd found myself that night likely wasn't a mecca for rich, ladder-climbing entrepreneurs.

No, on my first full night in and near Kingsley—tiniest of tiny Midwestern towns; seriously, blink and you'd miss it—I was surrounded by mostly young farmer looking types, a couple flirty women, and old men gathered around a table drinking frothy beer and talking about the good old days.

Ugh.

Gay bars in the city were so much easier. At least there I almost always knew a wink or a long glance or a lift of the chin meant something.

Here? A Shilesville or Kingsley wink or long glance or lift of the chin could mean anything. I knew I looked out of place. Surrounded by an overabundance of camo—really, *any* amount of camo was too much—flannel, and work boots, my dress pants, dress shirt, and dress shoes definitely stood out like a sore thumb. In my defense, I'd left for Kingsley straight from work—and I really didn't have any clothing that would have fit in anyway. Which was something I very likely needed to remedy as soon as possible. Pretty sure helping Gran run a bed and breakfast called for clothes that were decidedly *not* business attire—at least not the type of business clothes I owned.

Did all the patrons wonder who I was? Just some city slicker stopping by for a beer before traveling to the next flashy, luxurious destination? Or maybe the long glances were the result of me pinging a few homophobic radars?

Either way, I wasn't going back to Kingsley just yet. Even without a hookup, I needed a break and time to clear my head.

I scoffed into my beer. *A break?*

Hell, I'd been in Kingsley less than twenty-four hours—actually less than six hours—and I already needed a break?

Fuck. That didn't bode well for the next three months.

Three months.

It was *only* three months.

Double fuck.

Thank God I loved my Gran to the moon and back. Without my love and devotion for her, I probably would have already flown the coop. To where? I had no clue. Not like I could go back to Rockhurst. My apartment and job were in Rockhurst, but so were my father and Gramps. And Doctor Barret.

Gran, Gramps, and my father—how *that* asshole came from two amazing people I'd never know—had heard every word Doctor Barret, our family doctor and their close friend, had said about my health and immediately banished me to Kingsley.

Overworked.

Stressed.

Exhaustion.

Anxiety.

Working himself to death.

Doctor Barret hadn't held anything back in his assessment of my health—the appointment *wasn't* my idea, I was forced to attend—and his following summary of my health to my family didn't paint a pretty picture. Unfortunately, the whole crew had been in my office when I called Doc back to clarify a few things from the appointment. I'd thought maybe he'd tell me to get some more sleep and prescribe me a pill.

But, *no*. Not even close.

Doctor Barret said two months away from my high-stress sales management position. Dad had thrown a disgusted and disappointed glance my way and returned to his office. Gramps and Gran had glommed onto the idea and assured the doctor that I would get two full months away from Rockhurst and the stress of my job.

Two. Fucking. Months.

Gramps had assured me my bills and apartment would be covered despite my extended absence from work. I appreciated that. I had no wish to lose my glamorous apartment. But what in the hell was I going to do with myself if I wasn't at work twelve hours a day?

I wasn't given a warning or time to adjust to the sentencing. The day of my doctor visit, I went back to work to finish the day, but Gramps told me to gather my things and go home. Gran was already headed to Kingsley and expected me there within a day.

When my dear sister came to me in tears right before I left to let me know she'd screwed up *big time*, I assured her I'd take the blame and keep the heat off her. After all, I wasn't going to be there to get berated by my father. I swear, that man spent most of my life letting me know I was a colossal disappointment.

Maybe my father was right, maybe I was a complete idiot, because I certainly hadn't thought about how badly covering for Marissa would backfire.

"Marcus," Gramps had placed a strong but loving hand on my shoulder, "let's make it three months just for good measure. Within that time, we'll have your mistake cleared up, your dad will move on to being pissed at something else, and you'll have had a relaxing three months with Gran." He smiled. "She's looking so forward to your help and your company. I gotta tell you that I'm grateful you'll be there to help her. She still tries to do it all, but she's not as young as she once was. Knowing you're there will help ease my worry."

While my mind whirled and my gut churned, I couldn't help but smile fondly at the mention of Gran. She had spent forty years—my entire life plus another decade—running a seasonal bed and breakfast in her namesake town of Kingsley. Sure, the town was originally owned by and named after Gramps' grandparents and then his parents, but it was every bit as much Gran's town now.

"I seriously can't fathom how you've *never* been to Kingsley," Gramps muttered as we strode toward the bank of elevators. Our family business, Kingsley Sales and Logistics, took up the entire twenty-third floor and I couldn't believe I'd be gone from the place for three months.

Three. Fucking. Months.

"In thirty years, you've never gone to Kingsley even once?" Gramps continued.

"It's open March through September, right?" By *it*, I referred to the bed and breakfast. The town was obviously *open* and inhabited year-round for the most part.

Gramps nodded as the elevator opened.

"Spring was school, theater, and tennis. Summer was life guarding and interning. Fall was school and cross country. Then I was off to college. Never had time." I shrugged. Dad had been sure to keep me as busy as possible in hopes of *normalizing* me.

"But as a child? You never wanted to go with Marissa? She spent so much time in Kingsley. I guess I'm as bad as your father for not realizing you never went to visit." Gramps paused at the building exit.

"First, you are *nothing* like him." I shook my head. "Marissa was an introvert and book worm. I had a social life by the age of eight—even though it was forced on me. Before that, Mom and Dad were likely too busy screaming and hating each other to think I might want to go. Besides, I've never been one for a nature-filled, laid-back lifestyle." I wrinkled my nose. "Dad probably thought a BnB would make me even more gay, so he kept me busy with sports and socializing with his business partners' kids."

I'd been different—and known it—since a *very* young age. Despite my father doing his best to make me *normal*, I'd always embraced my true self and never hid who I was.

"Well, Gran is beside herself to get all this time with *just* you." Gramps pulled me into a hug—he never had fit the image of a business tycoon—and patted me on the back. "You rest and take it easy. This will all be here if and when you decide to come back."

"If?!" I'd squeaked, causing Gramps to chuckle. "Oh, I'm coming back. I'll be ready to scratch my eyes out just for something to do by the time three months is over. Probably by the time three *days are over*," I assured. "You know I don't do *downtime* well."

Gramps hummed. "Kingsley has a way of changing a person. You never know."

"Yeah, by making them die of boredom. I'm a city boy

through-and-through; there's no way I'm not coming back," I said.

"Don't be afraid to like the place."

"If it's so great, why didn't *you* stay?" I pushed.

"I don't trust your father to treat my employees right," Gramps answered with no hesitation. "If your Gran wanted to move there permanently, I'd pack my bags, work remotely, visit the city and office as needed, and never look back."

My eyes widened in response. "Really? You like Kingsley that much?"

He nodded. "I do. It gets in your blood; good for the heart and soul."

I'd never really known Gramps felt that way. "Well, Rockhurst is in *my* blood and this city boy is coming back after his three-month banishment."

Gramps had just nodded with a slight smile and gave me a wave as I'd headed out.

"You one of those beer readers or something?" a voice to my left pulled me from the memory.

"Huh?" I grunted as I turned to take in the hottest man in the bar—possibly one of the hottest men I'd ever seen. If you liked the rugged farmer type. Which I usually did *not* find myself attracted to, but this man was gorgeous with a kind smile to boot.

"Like a person reads tea leaves? Just wondered if you read beer. You were staring pretty intently into your mug for a long time; thought maybe you saw something in there." Hot country boy's kind smile hinted at something close to devastating. No, *boy* was the wrong word. *Man*. He was at least ten years older than me—evident by the laugh lines around his eyes and the slight silver in his chestnut hair—but his gleaming chocolate brown eyes and killer smile made him appear younger. He was just slightly taller than me, broader in the chest, but we shared a long, leanly muscled build.

"Nah, just lost in thought," I said.

Country boy gave a slight nod, his eyes meeting mine over his bottle of beer as he took a long swallow. When he shifted to lean against the bar and his elbow lightly brushed my arm, I took action—and prayed that *interested* translated in the country the same as it did in the city.

"You want to tell me your name and kill some time over a beer," I asked in a low voice, "or are we gonna keep our names to ourselves and get out of here?"

For one fleeting moment, as a look of shock crossed his face, I worried I'd overstepped and read the situation completely wrong. But then he schooled his features, drained the rest of his beer, and gave me a nod.

"I'd prefer to keep the names and get out of here," he said with a wink.

I tossed a bill down on the bar that would cover my two beers and a hefty tip. "Let's go."

When we reached the parking lot, I had to laugh at the line-up of vehicles. "I guess you can tell which one is mine." I indicated to the lone car in a sea of big pick-up trucks.

Country boy chuckled. "I'm guessing you're not from around here?"

I shook my head. "You live here?"

"Close enough," he answered. "We can take my truck." He gestured toward a shiny black Chevy Silverado.

I gave a nod and walked to the passenger side. Briefly, I thought of how different this was for me. Usually I was driving. Usually I took the guy to a hotel. Usually I got fucked and then left. But I shook the thoughts away. I was in a new place. No fancy hotels to go to. I'd have to trust country boy to get us where we were going. *Trust*. That word bounced in my head for a moment as I glanced toward him. Yeah, for some reason, I automatically trusted the man. Which was strange because I was often leery of new people.

But I had a good read on people in my line of work, so I'd learned to trust my gut.

"I'm guessing there aren't a lot of accommodations out this way?" I asked.

"No," he answered with an easy smile. "But I know a place."

We drove in a comfortable silence for a while.

"You pick guys up at that bar often?" I asked.

Country boy smiled, shyly this time, and shook his head. "No. I usually go a few towns farther away. There are some gay bars around—not many, but a couple. Honestly, I was just driving through tonight and wanted a beer before I went home. Saw you and something told me to say hello."

"Well, for a split second, I thought I'd totally blown it. Hookups in the city are a lot easier to read." I watched the trees, bathed in a soft glow from the full moon, rush by as the truck drove away from the bar. And away from my car. "You're not taking me out in the middle of nowhere to kill me, are you?" I joked with only the slightest tinge of real nervousness.

Country boy threw his head back and laughed. "You caught me. I'm a farmer by day and a serial killer by night."

His laughter loosened the sudden knot in my chest and I smiled. "Okay, okay. But I'm usually the one driving or we take an Uber, so the thought of being at your mercy and away from my vehicle has me a bit anxious."

He turned a comforting smile my way. "I can take you back to your car at any time. No questions asked." He cleared his throat. "I um, gotta be honest, I only do this *maybe* three or four times a year. So, I'm a little anxious myself."

My eyes grew wide. "For real? Wow. Guess we were in the right place at the right time, huh?"

He winced. "Well, maybe not totally *right* because I'm realizing I don't have any, um, *supplies.*"

For some reason, that fact both settled me and disappointed me. I didn't often have full-on penetrative sex with my hookups—at least not until we'd met up a couple times if it ever came to that—but the thought of bending over for the hot country boy had me completely turned on.

"No worries, we can do other stuff." I winked. "I'm completely clear, by the way. I get tested often and I'm always safe." My head told my dick it was for the best that my condoms and lube were safely in my luggage at the BnB.

Country boy swallowed and nodded. "Me too. Well, not tested *often*, but I've been tested since my last sexual encounter and all clear."

I watched the countryside roll by for a few moments. "So, where exactly are we going?" If he was taking me to his house, I was going to feel super awkward. I hadn't had sex in *my* bed—ever—and in anyone else's bed since a boyfriend in high school. Hotels and couches and showers were easier and a lot less intimate. Emotions were *not* part of my sexual encounters. I was an amazing—and maybe somewhat cold—business manager because I led my team with my head and not my heart. The same was true with the men I slept with—always best to keep intimacy and emotions out of the picture.

"Well, there's a secluded spot on the bluff," he began.

"What's a bluff?" I interrupted.

He cracked a smile. "It's kinda like a cliff. Little smaller, more round than the straight drop off. But this one borders a river. With luck, no one is there."

As he pulled the truck onto a gravel road, I gave a brief thought as to where our little encounter would actually take place. The ground? *Um, no.*

Almost as if he read my mind, my companion chuckled. "I've got some blankets in the back. We can spread them in the truck bed."

Blowjobs against the door would have been a bit less cozy,

but I wasn't going to argue with a soft blanket and the chance to keep the knees of my dress pants clean.

"Wouldn't want to mess up your fancy clothes," country boy quipped with a teasing grin.

I smiled. I really would need to get clothes and shoes better suited for country living and working at a bed and breakfast.

He pulled the truck onto a small path and maneuvered it behind a grove of trees on the right. To the left was a slight drop-off, a stone wall, and then what looked like a steep descent into what I'd guess was the river, although the bank was so grown up at the spot, I couldn't see any water.

"So, this is a bluff?" I asked.

"Yep," he nodded. "River is beyond those trees and down the embankment. There are other places along the river that are open and you can actually launch a boat and fish, but this is the most secluded point in this area." Country boy turned off the key and turned my way. "You still want to do this? No worries if you've changed your mind."

I nodded and opened my door. When he met me around the back of the truck and tossed a couple blankets into the truck bed, I smiled slightly. "Might as well give it a try, right? We can call it off if it's just not working?" By this point with other hookups, we'd likely have already made out in the hotel elevator and stumbled into the room in a tangled mess of lips, tongues, and arms. A hookup by the river was definitely out of my comfort zone.

"Call it quits at any time," country boy promised as he let down the tailgate of his truck. He turned toward me and ghosted a hand over my cheek before resting it on my shoulder.

With no hesitation, I stepped closer. Into his warmth, into his scent, and into a heady feeling of anticipation. I wrapped my arms around his neck and nuzzled my nose against his jaw. As my lips moved to hover over his, I whispered, "You okay with kissing?"

He moved to close the space and his warm, soft lips captured mine in a kiss that I expected to be gentle and enjoyable. I did *not* expect the zing of heat and electricity that traveled through me as his mouth owned mine.

I moaned into the kiss.

Moaned.

I was not a moaner when it came to kissing. Especially first kisses with complete strangers. But this man's mouth lit me on fire.

When his hands moved to grip my hips, I took a step even closer and rocked into him. The bulge behind his zipper pressed into my own erection, and we took advantage of the heat and friction as we continued to explore each other's mouths.

"Hand jobs? Blow jobs?" country boy asked gruffly as he broke the kiss.

My dick and ass screamed *Spread me out on your truck and fuck me hard and fast*, but my head scrambled to keep me thinking clearly. "Both? Either? Hell, I don't care."

In the bright moonlight, his face was just a shadow, but he smiled and licked his lips. "As great as it would be to get naked, we probably need to be ready to bolt at any moment."

"Clothed it is, then," I quipped. I reached for his jeans and made quick work of his button and zipper. Pushing his pants and underwear down just slightly, I wrapped my hand around his already hard, thick cock and pulled him out. I swallowed and fought the urge to drop to my knees, gravel and dirt be damned.

Country boy mirrored my movements and soon we were kissing, hot and deep, while we stroked each other as we stood in the moonlight. "Want to stay here or stretch out?" he asked.

I moved to sit on the tailgate as my companion reached to spread out the blankets. Once we'd both shifted to the middle of the truck bed, he leaned in to resume the kiss. As badly as my dick wanted his mouth, I couldn't help but savor the heated and desperate kisses.

Country boy pulled back, breathing hard. "Sorry, I'm not usually so into kissing, but your mouth is insane."

I nipped at his lip and licked the spot with my tongue. "Just wait until you see what I can do with your dick," I teased.

With some very unsexy and awkward maneuvering, we ended up stretched out on our sides in the classic sixty-nine position. As amazing as complete nakedness would have been—who wouldn't want to have full-body skin-to-skin contact with this guy's gorgeous body?—I appreciated the clothing-on option in case other visitors to the bluff arrived. And the fact that we at least had access to each other's balls and cocks was enough. This was a quickie with a guy I'd never see again—I didn't need romance or foreplay.

I nuzzled my nose against his groin and breathed in his intoxicating scent. If I'd been at all interested in a relationship, I would have definitely considered claiming him as mine and bottling his scent so I could wear it all day and be wrapped in his arms all night. *Jesus. What the fuck was that? Creeper.*

Before I could push the thought from my head, his warm, wet mouth engulfed my dick and I growled as I rocked forward to give him more. Within seconds, I took his thick cock into my mouth and swirled my tongue around the head. I savored the tangy flavor of him as I tongued his slit and breathed through my gag reflex when I took him deep to the back of my throat.

For several moments, we stroked and licked and sucked.

Holy shit. Did all country boys suck dick this well? Again, the thought of taking him to the BnB just to keep him around for sex crossed my ready-to-bust-a-nut mind. I pushed the thought away and focused on his dick and my impending orgasm.

"Fuck, your mouth is fucking magic," he murmured briefly before taking me back into his heat.

We fucked around for a few more moments before the intensity of what we were doing got to be too much. Our hips thrust. Once, twice, three times before we both hummed around the throbbing cocks in our mouths and unloaded onto each other's tongues.

For a brief moment, I saw stars and wanted to move to curl into his chest and beg him for another round. But I pushed away the ridiculousness of that idea and wiped his cum from the corner of my mouth.

Country boy shifted so that our spent cocks were level and our mouths came together in a soft, but no-less-hot, kiss. "You really do have a magic mouth. That was amazing," he whispered gruffly.

"Agreed." I smacked a kiss against his lips and tucked myself back into my dress pants. "And barely a speck of dirt on me." I winked and scooted to the end of the truck bed before hopping off the tailgate and straightening my clothes.

A look I couldn't read flitted across his face, but it was gone before I could even attempt to analyze it. "Better head back to your car. I think we lucked out with no interruptions."

I walked toward the passenger door while he gathered the blankets and tossed them behind the seat. "Just as well. I wasn't looking forward to panicking and running away before we got to the good part."

He laughed and started the truck.

We made a bit of small talk on the way back to the bar,

but mostly I spent the time thinking about how much less awkward it was to send a hookup home in an Uber.

"Well, here we are," he said as he pulled up behind my car. "You wanna go in and get a drink?" His offer seemed genuine, but mostly because he wasn't sure how to end our encounter.

"Nah, I need to get going," I said with my hand on the door handle.

"Yeah," he agreed with a nod, "probably have big business to attend to. Finance meetings, presentations, hiring and firing."

I chuckled a bit at his presumptions of what I did. He wasn't *entirely* wrong. But I figured he could think what he wanted about my city boy job. No reason to let him know I was actually heading to the little town of Kingsley to help my grandmother run a seasonal bed and breakfast for three months. And not by choice.

With a hookup *that* good in the city, I would have definitely been hinting at exchanging numbers. We could fuck each other's brains out for a week or so until the heat fizzled. But I was now living in the middle of nowhere with Gran. My goal was to survive the three months and hightail it out of there as quickly as possible. No need for connections with extracurriculars.

"Yep. Better get to it." I started to open the door, but for some reason felt compelled to say *something* else. Anything. "Tonight was really good. Another time, another place? I'd definitely be down for a repeat. Take care." I climbed from the truck, but not before I saw the smile and blush cross his face.

"DID YOU HAVE A NICE TIME?" Gran asked when I let myself in the back door of the BnB. We wouldn't have guests for a week or so, but preparations were well underway for the Spring Grand Opening.

"Yeah, nice to just get away and clear my head," I said as I gave her a hug.

"Well, you just got here, so I'm not sure what you needed to *get away* from. And you smell like you've been outside most the night." Gran eyed me up and down and I panicked she was going to know what I'd been doing.

I wasn't used to answering to anyone outside of work. At my job, I answered to Dad and Gramps. But mostly, people answered to me. In my personal life, I answered to only myself. Living with Gran and a houseful of strangers was going to be a definite adjustment.

"We need to get you some work clothes. Unless you brought something more suitable for hard work and country living?" Gran asked as she studied my dress shoes.

"No, I will need to order some things or go shopping. Is there even a mall around here?"

Gran snorted. "Won't find a mall; at least not nearby. Not that most malls sell the type of clothes you'll need. Busy, busy day tomorrow. You'll have to make do with what you've got. But the day after, you can go get what you'll need."

"Will I need to go to the general store and buy sturdy cloth for you to sew me some trousers?" I teased. "Maybe I can ask the old man at the mercantile counter if he can refer me to a shoemaker? Will you need me to pick up your order of sugar and flour and penny candy?"

Gran smacked me on the shoulder. "Funny, funny boy."

A growing rumble and shrill sound shattered the air and I winced. Kingsley was near a railroad and, while the trains didn't stop or load in the town, they did have to blow their whistle as a safety measure when they rumbled through.

"I don't know *how* you think a person can sleep with that damn train whistle going by multiple times a day," I grumbled. "It's annoying as hell."

"You get used to it. I almost find it soothing." Gran patted my cheek. "We're up at dawn."

I rolled my eyes. *Dawn*? How early was that? I'd set my alarm for eight. If it wasn't early enough, I'd claim ignorance when Gran came after me.

Little did I know.

TWO

JORDAN MOORE

I COULDN'T WIPE the goofy smile from my face. Throughout my morning chores—feeding the chickens, gathering eggs, tending the vegetable gardens—I knew I was blushing and grinning as I thought about the night before. And I couldn't even care.

The city boy I'd run into at the Shilesville bar was hot as sin.

My first thought when I'd seen him was that there was *no way* a gay guy from the city was in a tiny bar in the middle of nowhere—actually, the first thought that ran through my head was that he looked terribly familiar. Probably because he looked like he'd just stepped from a magazine or a television show. But then I gave myself permission to think he'd stopped by for a beer between busy, serious, fancy job Point A and luxurious, professional, successful Destination B.

Don't get me wrong. I adored my home in Kingsley. I'd lived there most of my life and taken over the family farm upon my parents' deaths when I was thirty. I'd been running the poultry farm and vegetable gardens along with my carpentry and general handyman business for ten years and figured I'd spend the rest of my life in the postage-stamp-sized town.

But thinking about the gorgeous city boy—okay, he was for sure younger than me, but not *that* much—made me imagine his life as all that Kingsley wasn't. I had no desire to live in the city—mostly because I'd never been and I had no clue what I'd do there—but picturing him in his suit and tie, all serious in a boardroom, taking men to pricey, luxurious hotels or to his glamorous penthouse apartment had me thinking maybe the city wasn't so bad.

That gentle brush of my arm against his had been the only move I needed to make before he took control. I hated that the best I could give him was a blow job by the river, but Shilesville—the town next to Kingsley—didn't have a hotel. And it wasn't like I could take him back to Kingsley and ask Ellie if I could use one of her bed and breakfast rooms.

I'd never had a man in my bed. I'd never brought a man to my house.

Ellie was a dear friend and I missed her when she wasn't in Kingsley. She was the only person in my life who knew without a doubt that I was gay. And I loved her for not blinking an eye. Others in town probably suspected, but I wasn't sure I wanted or needed to confirm their suspicions. I went a couple hours away three, maybe four, times a year to scratch an itch. That was enough.

Or so I told myself.

A gay poultry and vegetable farmer with skills in carpentry and general fix-it jobs announcing he was gay, finding a loving partner who *wanted* to live in Kingsley, and settling in for a happily ever after?

Yeah, right.

My chest gave a squeeze. Didn't mean I would stop dreaming about it. But I knew that it wasn't my reality. So, I gave in and searched out anonymous hookups from time-to-time, and enjoyed my simple life the rest of the time. It worked for me.

Until last night.

The heat.

The connection—albeit somewhat awkward.

The way I'd floated home.

None of that had ever happened before.

There was something about the dark-blond man, his blue eyes twinkling and his soft lips smiling, that drew me in and made me want *more*.

I snorted. "Moore is your last name and that's all you're getting," I grumbled as I picked tomatoes from the indoor hothouse plants.

But that didn't mean I would ever forget about my encounter the night before. I'd be jerking off to that city boy for years to come.

After washing the vegetables—starting the hothouse gardens had been a genius idea and I was able to keep Kingsley in fresh veggies all year—I packed up the baskets that I'd drop at the local farmers market along with baskets for the grocer. I set up quite a few options at the little stand at the end of my driveway. The veggies would be gone by the end of the day and my little cash bucket would have a decent haul in it. Kingsley as a whole was an honest bunch of people and payment for my products almost always made their way into the bucket. I did appreciate the people who dropped envelopes of cash into my mail slot, but I trusted most to put a fair amount in the bucket as payment for their picks.

I washed my hands and piled the veggie baskets into my sleek, black truck—probably one of the only things I'd ever splurged on—and headed to do my drop-offs before I went to Ellie's.

Ellen Kingsley was a fixture in this town and her bed and

breakfast was booked solid from March until September. She was also my best friend. Something about the woman and I just clicked. I had a sister and some nieces and nephews who came to visit. I was friendly with most everyone in town. But Ellie was my one true friend.

We often had tea and cake dates—who cared that it was before seven in the morning? Ellie had convinced me that life was too short and if we wanted tea and cake for breakfast, so be it. We'd enjoy our chat and then get busy with our business plans for the bed and breakfast.

Ellie's Bed and Breakfast was the best for miles around and she worked hard to keep it that way. I loved helping her with repairs and creating new items—last year she had me make the new dining room table and chairs—and just assisting with the preparations in general.

We were *neighbors* in the sense that Ellie's place was the closest house to mine. Yes, it was a little under a quarter mile away, but when you lived out in the middle of nowhere, that was *close*.

After driving past Ellie's to drop off the day's veggies at the market and grocery, I pointed the truck toward the bed and breakfast with a smile. I knew the visit would bring delicious food, great conversation, and a to-do list a mile long. It would also pad my savings—Ellie's bed and breakfast kept me in business and cash for most of the year.

Ellie greeted me at the door with a big hug. "Jordan Moore, you are a sight for sore eyes. Get in here. I've got tea and cake ready."

I took a deep breath and sighed. "Good to have you *home*," I said as the scent of cinnamon, bread, and cleaning supplies filled my nose.

"So glad to be back. I'm itching to get started on fixes, touch-ups, and opening preparations." Ellie brought a huge platter of cinnamon rolls to the table as I took a seat.

"Decided to try a new recipe, so we're having cinnamon rolls instead of cake." She bustled back to the counter to pour hot water in mugs. "Got a new loose-leaf black tea, too. You'll be my tester."

"Not going to hear a complaint from me."

We settled in for breakfast and all was right in my world.

"Well, tell me what you've been up to," Ellie said.

Had amazing sex last night with a complete stranger I'll never see again. I took a sip of tea to hide my smile. "Just the usual. Added a few new chickens. My old rooster died—not surprising, he was ancient—so I replaced him. The new guy is a bit cantankerous. Definitely thinks morning is a lot earlier than the old guy." I laughed.

Ellie smiled over her tea cup. "Mmhm, I've noticed. It's all part of country living. Between the train and the rooster, I'm sure M…"

Her words were cut off by thumping feet on the stairs. "Gran, there is no way I can sleep with that damn train. And who has a fucking rooster? That fucker crowed at the ass-crack of dawn and every five minutes since."

When the face with the voice appeared, I sucked a bite of cinnamon roll down my throat and sputtered to recover.

City boy.

In Ellie's kitchen.

Calling her *Gran*.

Oh, holy fuck.

His eyes went wide just as Ellie admonished, "Language, Marcus."

Marcus.

He drew up short and quickly schooled his features. "Sorry, Gran." He glanced my way. "I apologize. I didn't realize we had guests already." His cheeks flushed.

"Marcus, I'd like you to meet one of my very closest

friends, Jordan Moore." Ellie gestured toward me. "Jordan, this is my grandson, Marcus Kingsley."

He'd recovered somewhat and stepped forward to shake my hand. "Marc is fine."

Heat zinged through my skin when our hands touched.

"*This* is Mr. Moore?" Marc asked. "I thought he was some old guy."

"Guilty." I smiled. "Older than you at least." I turned to Ellie. "You haven't shown me pictures of your grandkids grown up, I was still picturing Marcus and Marissa as ten years old." My gut clenched. I guess there was a reason the guy had looked somewhat familiar last night.

Ellie waved us off. "Let's get started on the plans. Marcus, you'll be working with Jordan most of today on repairs and touch-ups. Then, after you get some more suitable clothes tomorrow, I'll expect you to be his right hand of sorts. Like an assistant. He'll need your help with his farm along with all the BnB preparations."

Marc's eyes grew wide. "I can help *you*. I thought you were excited about having me here?"

"Oh, I'll be planning grocery lists, menus, and to-do lists a mile long when I'm not confirming reservations and cleaning schedules." Ellie handed her grandson a plate along with a cup of tea. "When you're not helping Jordan, you can help me. But you'll be most useful with him. And we're living together, so we'll see plenty of each other."

With Ellie pretty much shutting down any and all arguments Marcus may have wanted to give her, we settled in for planning and preparations. About ten minutes into Ellie and I discussing the water pump she wanted to install on the patio, a loud rooster crow filled the air.

I winced.

Ellie chuckled.

Marcus growled. "Seriously, who has the damn rooster? It needs to be barbecued."

"Marcus!" Ellie scolded. "That's Jordan's rooster. It's a part of his poultry farm. You'll just have to get used to it. Country living," she chirped with a smile.

"Sorry about that. Hank has a much earlier internal alarm clock than my old rooster." I shrugged. "At least you're here and not right next to it. First morning he crowed scared the shit out of me."

Marcus narrowed his eyes and huffed. "Fabulous. Do you *really* expect me to be up at the ass-crack of dawn?"

Ellie gave him a look. "Yes, I do. You're here and I expect you to pull your weight. The fresh air and physical work will be healthy."

Marcus sighed, but nodded as if giving in to something unspoken. He turned his blue eyes my way. "What time do you want my help?"

"Can you be over to my house in an hour?" I figured I'd start by showing him the farm work and then we'd move on to the bed and breakfast prep.

"He'll be there," Ellie interrupted. "I know you two are going to be a great team."

Marcus squinted at his grandmother, but gave me a nod. "Yeah, I'll be over in a bit. Just need to change." He gestured to the t-shirt and silk pants I assumed he'd slept in.

My traitorous dick twitched as I thought about what his silk-covered body would feel like under my hands. I'd had an up-close and personal encounter with the guy's cock and I wanted more. Instead, I sipped my tea while sitting at his grandmother's kitchen table and making plans to show last night's hookup how to pick tomatoes, peppers, and green beans.

"Since you'll likely be over there most of the day, I'll send food. Why don't you boys plan to be back here by seven for a late dinner." Ellie pushed back from the table. "You can fill me in on how productive your day was."

Marcus excused himself, presumably to go change.

I stood. "Thanks for the goodies. Tell Marcus," I cleared my throat and corrected myself, "*Marc*, that I'll be waiting."

Ellie gave me a hug. "So glad to be back here. It truly is home, you know?" She patted my face. "My grandson is going to need work clothes. Perhaps that can be first on tomorrow's agenda?"

"Oh, um, yeah. Sure." She wanted me to take him *shopping*? "I can take him after morning chores tomorrow and get him all set up. I'm guessing those dress pants aren't made for digging in a vegetable garden."

Ellie narrowed her eyes. "What dress pants?"

I froze. "Um, he works in the city, right? I'd assume he wears nice dress pants?"

She pursed her lips and nodded. "Marcus needs this place. The location, the slower pace, the people. He doesn't realize it yet, but he does. It's in his blood and I have every intention of making sure he finds himself here." She smiled softly. "If we give him enough to love, he'll have no choice but to stay."

"He's lived his entire life in the hustle and bustle of Rockhurst? He has a successful career with Kingsley Sales and Logistics, right?" I cocked my head.

Ellie nodded.

"Then what makes you think he'd ever want to move to a tiny country town?"

"Kingsley has a way of getting to people." She winked. "And something tells me that Marcus will eventually figure out just how lonely he is in Rockhurst."

"And he'd not be lonely in a town of less than five hundred?" I smirked.

"Doesn't matter how many people are around you if you can find the right person," she answered with her own smirk.

"Show him what this town has to offer. Show him what he'd be missing out on if he leaves."

I frowned. "Pretty sure me showing him how to sand a board or gather some eggs isn't going to be enough to keep him here."

"May have to go a bit deeper than that," Ellie answered and turned to gather the dishes from the table. "I'll send the food with Marcus."

As I drove home, I found my head a jumbled mess. Marcus—my hot city boy hookup—was my best friend's grandson. He was only in Kingsley for a short time. My best friend seemed to think I could make him stay. And Marcus appeared to be highly disgruntled about working with me.

I ran a hand over my face.

Definitely not the way I'd thought the day was going to go.

THREE

MARC

I FOUND an old flannel shirt in the closet; I assumed it belonged to Gramps. But I was out of luck for pants and shoes. I yanked on my most casual dress pants and rolled my eyes. I looked absolutely ridiculous in a flannel shirt and black dress pants.

Who do you need to impress? You're going to be doing manual labor; it's not like you're walking into a club.

Jordan's deep brown eyes came to mind.

Did I need to impress him? Did I care what he thought?

Scenes from last night flitted through my mind. His gorgeous eyes and smile. That simple brush of his arm against me. The somewhat sweet and refreshing awkwardness we muddled through in the truck. His mouth. That damn electric kiss. The heat of his tongue swirling around my cock. His dick thrusting between my lips.

Holy fuck. I palmed myself and attempted to calm down.

What the hell was going on?

How the fuck did I end up banished to Kingsley and hook up with the one guy I definitely shouldn't have? There were so many issues with my current situation and I was having trouble sorting through everything.

I stared at my choice of shoes. I'd worn my oldest pair of Oxfords to travel to Kingsley. I'd also brought a dressier pair —no clue why—and two pairs of fashion sneakers. The sneakers were newer and pricier than the old Oxfords. I'd *maybe* have more occasions to wear the sneakers than the dress shoes. The Oxfords would be maybe somewhat easier to clean and I could replace them if needed.

With a huff, I pulled on the Oxfords. I looked like one of those mismatch animal books where the top half and bottom half are all mixed up. But I had no other choice. Tomorrow, I'd get some clothes so I could at least save my own duds and maybe somewhat *look* the part.

Today?

Today I was heading to Jordan's house.

Jordan.

Gran's good friend.

Jordan.

The man whose cock I sucked last night.

Jordan.

The man who kissed me like I'd never been kissed.

I took a deep breath and blew it out slowly.

How were we going to approach this situation? Did we need to discuss last night? Did Gran know Jordan was gay? Did he know I was only here for three months? Did it matter? Would he want a repeat of last night? Did *I* want a repeat of last night?

So much for a trip to Kingsley helping to clear my head and improve my health. At this rate, I would end up more stressed than I was back in Rockhurst.

Because of a drop-dead gorgeous carpenter and poultry farmer. Although, as I paused at the top of the stairs, I noticed I didn't have my usual morning pounding headache. With the crappy night of sleep I got, I was sure it was a total coincidence.

I thumped down the stairs as a train blew its whistle. "You really don't hear that?" I asked Gran.

She smiled as she packed a picnic basket. "I hear it, but it doesn't bother me. It's just a comforting background noise. I miss it when I'm in the city."

"Do you miss Rockhurst when you're here?"

Gran pursed her lips and shook her head. "No, this is my home. Gramps is the only thing keeping me tied to the city."

"He said he'd live here full-time if you wanted," I offered.

She smiled. "I know. He's so good to me. When he retires, we'll live here. Or do the bed and breakfast March through September and maybe we'll do winters somewhere tropical." She placed some silverware wrapped in napkins into the basket. "The internet here isn't set up for all he'd need for work—it *could* be, but he doesn't want to bring his work life here. So, he visits and we make it work. I'm blessed that he understands my need to be here."

I smiled. "Gramps is one of the good ones, for sure." I fiddled with the loose button on my shirt. "So, how do I get to Jordan's?"

"Well, you're probably the most uniquely dressed helper he's ever had," Gran teased with a wink. She turned and pointed out the window. "See that house and barn? That's Jordan's place. You could walk, but since you're taking the picnic basket, I'd suggest you drive."

"Why did I think *Mr. Moore* was an old man?" I mused as Gran finished her packing.

She shrugged. "He's older than you, but only by about ten years. He's a wonderful person, Marcus. He adores his life here, but he's lonely. I think you two will be great friends."

"Gran, I'm only here for three months. I wasn't sent here to make friends. Plus, it kinda sucks to get friendly and then leave." I picked up the basket.

"Maybe it's worse to avoid getting friendly and miss out on something good."

"You and Gramps seem to think I'm going to want to stay here," I started, "but you guys *know* that I'm dedicated to Kingsley Sales and Logistics. Rockhurst is my home. That's not going to change." I felt like I needed to make sure they both knew that and weren't crushed when I left.

"*Home* is where the heart is," Gran quipped.

"And my *heart* is in Rockhurst. My job, my apartment, my friends are there." It felt like I *had* to argue, even though my job, my apartment, my *friends* were definitely not part of anything resembling my heart. I didn't let my heart get involved in things like that. Hell, I didn't let my heart get involved in much of anything.

"A job you can do from anywhere. An apartment that you barely live in. And friends that you keep at arm's length because you never really let anyone in." Gran pointed a finger at me. "Marcus, you're a mixture of your father and Gramps —and that's really good in many ways. But the city brings out the worst of your father in you. My hope for this extended stay is that you'll discover more of your Gramps side and realize that you're aloof, alone, and mostly just phoning it in when it comes to life and love."

"Love?" I snorted. "So, you think I'm going to fall in love and decide that my life's calling is to move to Kingsley and run a bed and breakfast with my Gran? I love you and this is a cute little town, but I need more than that."

"My hope is that you'll open yourself up to new possibilities, let down the walls, and maybe find something deeper than the superficial business relationships and empty booty calls you hide behind in Rockhurst." Gran's eyes were sharp and challenging.

I fought a blush over the fact the old woman knew about my meaningless sex life. She wasn't *wrong*, but I wasn't going there. Not right then.

"Where is all of this coming from?" I asked.

"Over the past year, I've really seen a side of you that reminds me too much of your father. I messed up with him. I didn't speak up. I didn't intervene. I'm not going to stand by and watch my grandson go down the same road." She crossed her arms over her chest. "I want to see you happy. In love, living your best life. Living your *real* life. Rockhurst isn't that for you."

"And Kingsley is?"

She shrugged. "I guess we'll see. I think Kingsley has what you're missing."

"A rude rooster, loud-ass train, and you?" I smirked. "Don't get me wrong. I love you to death, but I don't know that I'd stay here just for you."

"Wouldn't ask you to. I think there's more here than you realize. Maybe you'll open your eyes and your heart to possibilities and see what you think at the end of three months." She gave me a little shove. "Now, get going. Jordan is waiting."

I TOOK a deep breath and rolled my eyes at Jordan's failed attempt to hide his laughing smile when I got out of the truck. "Yeah, yeah, I know I look ridiculous. I don't have farm boy clothes; this is the best I could do."

"Them's mighty fancy shoes," Jordan drawled in a terrible stereotype of a country accent, "sure would be keen to get me some purty shoes like them there."

"Ha ha," I deadpanned. "Oxfords are a given in a business office environment."

"Ohhh, they even have a fancy name? *Oxfords*," he said as if trying out the word. "Very upscale." He gave a wink and I scolded myself for the butterflies in my stomach. "Well, let's get started, Oxford."

"My name is Marc."

"Marc, Marcus, Oxford, I like them all," Jordan answered with a teasing smirk.

I rolled my eyes and fell into step beside him. "Should we discuss last night?"

"Nope," Jordan answered. "Now, the vegetable gardens have to be tended daily in the growing season, usually twice a day, or they will get overgrown and I lose crop to rot or growing too big." He gestured toward two large areas filled with what I realized must have been tiny vegetable plants. "I got a really good start on the garden this year. As long as there's no freaky late frost, I should have a good crop come summer. But my bread and butter right now comes from the hothouse garden veggies." He pointed to what looked like a greenhouse. "That's where we'll start."

"Are you sure?" I pushed the issue of last night as I followed him to the greenhouse. "I'm here for three months. *Only* three months, but it seems like we should maybe clear the air about last night." Usually, I was all for the chance to move on with absolutely no strings and no discussion. For some reason—maybe because I'd be seeing Jordan every day —I wanted to talk about it.

"No need. It happened. It's over. We both knew it was a one-off and planned to never look back. That doesn't have to change." He opened the door and ushered me inside before moving to the edge of the indoor garden where several rows of corn stood tall and proud—I at least recognized corn. "You have to know when the corn is right to pick." He launched into a long explanation and demonstration of which ears of corn were ready to pick and which needed more time.

I listened and truly did attempt to store the information while still stuck on the *last night* issue. When he moved to the tomato plants, I huffed out a frustrated breath. "Yeah, but we planned on moving on and never looking back when we thought we'd never see each other again. Today is different. Today, you're my Gran's best friend. Today, I'll be working with you for three months. Today, you're not someone I can just forget about."

Jordan's eyes crinkled with a smile. "It was pretty unforgettable, huh?"

I rolled my eyes, but couldn't help returning the smile. "It was great. But that's not what I mean." I stepped into the little raised garden plot to look through a tomato plant for ripe fruit like I'd seen Jordan do—and my shoe sank into thick mud. "Fuck."

"Whoa there, Oxford," Jordan teased. "Some parts of the garden are a bit muddier than others—that applies to the indoor plots *and* outdoors."

I flipped him off. "I figured these were going to be ruined anyway." I found a red tomato and removed it from the plant like Jordan had instructed. Holding it up with a proud smile, I placed it in the basket Jordan was toting around. "Does Gran know you're gay?" I paused. "I mean, you *are* gay? Bi?"

Jordan chuckled and quickly added five tomatoes to the basket before I found even one more. "Ellie knows I'm gay. Most of the town doesn't. I'd assume they have their suspicions, but it's not something I've ever announced."

"Would they have a problem with it?" I asked.

Jordan pursed his lips before shaking his head. "No, I don't think so. I'd still be the local carpenter, handyman, vegetable supplier, and poultry farmer. As long as I continued doing my job, I don't think most would have a problem. I'd likely lose a bit of business, but nothing to devastate my income."

"So, you don't date?" I gently put another tomato in the basket.

Jordan moved us to the two long rows of green beans and showed me how to pick them. "Whatever we pick in here during the off months gets doubled and tripled when the outdoor gardens are in full bloom." He handed me a large cloth bag. "Put them in here." Jordan squatted down to begin picking beans. "No, I don't date. There's a very small pool of gay men in Kingsley," he chuckled, "and by small pool I mean *me* as far as I'm aware. I'm good with meaningless hookups a few times a year. The world—or at least *my world*—doesn't revolve around sex."

I let the subject drop for the time being because it sounded like Jordan had reached his irritation point. I didn't want to piss him off on my first day helping him and Gran. But for some strange reason, I couldn't get the *meaningless* hookups comment out of my head. That's all it had been for me, as well. That's all sex *ever* was for me. So, why did I have some weird desire to prove to Jordan that what we had together last night may have been temporary, but definitely wasn't meaningless? *Would you have felt the same if you were back in Rockhurst after a night like last night?* I rolled the thought around for a while. Being face-to-face with Jordan for sure made the situation different, but if I was being honest with myself, I think I would have let myself linger over thoughts of our hookup even if I'd been back in the city.

We quietly picked green beans for several moments—and I quickly discovered picking green beans was a terrible job that should be used as punishment for the very worst criminal offenders; the air inside the hothouse was, well, *hot*.

"This job isn't fun. I can't imagine how bad it will be in the heat of summer."

"That's why getting up when Hank crows is a good idea," Jordan joked. "The earlier you can get the veggies picked, the cooler the job." He shrugged with a bit of an odd look. "Plus, not a worry for you. You're only here for three months, so you'll miss the full gardens and heat of summer."

The thought of that struck me like a double-sided club. On one hand, I'd be back to my life in the city. On the other hand, it kinda stung. I glanced toward the barely-sprouted outdoor gardens and gave an inward shrug. Did I really care about some plants? No. It was ridiculous to think I'd be bent out of shape because I didn't get to see a vegetable garden in full bloom. Clearly, I was missing out on oxygen in the hothouse or something because my brain wasn't functioning correctly.

"Right. Luck's on my side," I replied as I handed my bag full of green beans to Jordan and followed him to another raised garden plot.

"Okay, these are zucchinis." He went about lifting leaves to show me the flower blooms and the zucchinis. "Now, this one here is pretty much ready, but I'm going to leave it to show you what one day can do if we don't pick often enough."

"One day can make a difference?" I raised a brow.

"Definitely." Jordan chuckled. "Funny story. When I was about fourteen, I decided to start a community garden in town. I got permission from the library to use their open lot. Plenty of people said they were interested in pitching in, but in the end, it was pretty much just me doing all the work. The librarian—she passed a few years before my parents—would help on Tuesday and Thursday, but I went to town three days a week and every weekend to work on that damn garden."

"Wait, you rode your bike all the way to town?"

Jordan snorted. "*All the way* isn't that far, but no, I drove."

"At fourteen?"

"This isn't Rockhurst and it was different back then. I was driving at thirteen. Anyway, I was super proud of my garden. I definitely got my parents' green thumb, but this was *mine* and not just the fruits of my parents' labor. So, I pushed aside that the whole *community garden* thing turned out to be *me* doing all the work. My first zucchini was beautiful. I spotted it on a Friday and knew it would be the perfect size by Saturday morning. Morning came and I rushed into town. Only to find old man Jenkins rummaging through the garden filling a bag like a pirate pilfering for treasure." Jordan's eyes danced as he told the story. "Jenkins finished his collection just as I was approaching and he gave a grunt and a wave and walked away—to be honest, he didn't get *much*—since the garden wasn't in full set, but I was still indignant." He chuckled. "I remember rushing to check on my zucchini and finding it gone. *He picked my freakin' zucchini*, I indignantly reported to Miss Agnes, the librarian."

I snorted. "There's a joke in there somewhere."

Jordan smiled. "Miss Agnes, tiny little thing with a slumped back, beady eyes, and bird beak nose, crossed her arms, eyed me up and down, and said," he paused as a bubble of laughter erupted, "she said, *Boy, a lot of men are gonna pick your zucchini over the years. Just gotta be sure which ones are deserving of the prize.*"

"Oh my God, no she didn't," I said.

Jordan laughed again. "God, I hadn't thought about that for years. At the time, I just thought she was a batty old woman nattering on with nonsense. But now, I'm wondering if she had an inkling about me even way back then. Of course, *I* had an inkling way back then, but I fought it tooth and nail, so I definitely didn't pick up on any innuendo—whether she meant it on purpose or not."

"Well," I waggled my brow, "was she right? Have plenty of men *picked your freakin' zucchini* over the years?"

Jordan blushed. "Plenty? Maybe not. But enough." His gaze caught mine for the briefest of moments before he glanced away. "The bigger issue is finding the one deserving of the prize." Jordan's words were quiet and he turned around to study one of the plants.

A strange energy buzzed through my body at his words. But I pushed it aside. I was there to help Gran and Jordan. I needed to assist with the BnB and *pick freakin' zucchinis*—and I meant that in the most literal way.

I shot one more look toward the vegetable Jordan had proclaimed *ready* and wondered just how much it would truly change in one day. I shrugged inwardly; he was the expert.

Once Jordan deemed our veggie picking done, we left the greenhouse—and I savored the cooler, fresh air—and headed to a large chicken coop.

"I let the chickens have free range for the most part, but they all have spots in the coop. I gather eggs in the morning and sometimes a couple times throughout the day. Some of my hens are more productive layers than others."

I frowned. "This is going to sound dumb—total city boy talking here—but how do you know which eggs are going to be chicks and which are just to eat?" It was a question I'd never even considered. When I bought eggs at the store, I *knew* they came from chickens, but the actual process had never really crossed my mind.

Jordan smiled and explained patiently. "That's why I only have two broody-hens and I collect eggs sometimes as many as three times a day. Since I do have the male presence with Hank, it's always a possibility that the eggs have been fertilized, but as long as they aren't incubated—by a hen sitting on them or artificial heat—they won't develop into chicks. Only my broody-hens make a habit of incubating eggs. The rest are more interested in laying an egg and then going back out in the yard to find food. I make half my chicken money from selling eggs and half from selling broilers." I must have looked confused because he explained. "Broilers, fryers, roasters...they're chickens used for meat. They don't produce as many eggs a year as layers."

I eyed the chickens. "What do they eat?"

"Since they are free-range, I feed them only small amounts of chicken feed. They mostly eat bugs, seeds, leaves, and grasses." Jordan opened the coop and pointed to the two sides. "Over on the left is where my broody-hens will usually sit on eggs in hopes they hatch. My layers usually lay theirs over here," he pointed to the right, "which makes it easy to gather them."

"What if the broody-hens are sitting on unfertilized eggs?" I was still trying to follow the process in my head.

"If the broody-hens' eggs don't hatch after twenty-one days, I have to toss them because they'd only start to grow bacteria." Jordan began picking up eggs from the hen boxes. "I usually try to make sure the broodies and Hank get some one-on-one time together," he winked. "That way I'll know there's a better chance of the eggs hatching. I can't assure Hank doesn't get with the others, but he seems pretty happy with his conjugal visits with the two broodies."

I chuckled. "So, you're like a chicken pimp."

Jordan threw his head back and laughed. "I guess you could say that."

We took a break to wash our hands, get drinks, and stock the roadside veggie stand.

"I can't believe you just leave the produce out here and people put money in a bucket." I shook my head in disbelief. "I'm surprised you're not robbed daily."

"Nah, Kingsley is a pretty honest bunch overall."

"That will definitely take some getting used to," I muttered as I continued to stare at the bucket of cash. "I can just see some city people driving through here and taking selfies with the veggie stand and cash bucket. They'd post on social media about the quaint little town where buckets of cash for veggie payment was the norm and how adorable and cute and rustic it was." I kinda rolled my eyes at the image.

"Is that what you're thinking?" Jordan elbowed me.

"I mean, maybe? It's so far out of my box that it definitely strikes me as almost crazy. But the more I think about it, the more irritated I'd probably be at the big deal they'd make over it." And what the hell did that even mean?

"You oughtta see how excited they get over chickens. And they'll tag Ellie's page over and over about the *precious* country tea cups and décor, the *downhome* country cooking, the *rustic* hikes and boating excursions." Jordan laughed. "It's all part of the experience, but it can get a little annoying. Like, this is our home and our life. It's not a vacation for the folks of Kingsley. We love Ellie's place and we're grateful for the tourists and vacationers because they fund our little town for much of the year. But sometimes it *does* feel like we're just some country hicks on display for other people's pleasure." He sighed. "I don't know if that makes sense."

I followed him to what looked like a garage or workshop. "Two days ago, I don't think it would have. Today? For some odd reason, I get it." How had I become protective of the little town in such a short time? "I guess, in a way, it's like when non-city people come to visit the city and snap pictures and talk about how different city-life is than wherever they're from."

Jordan nodded. "Yeah, I can see that." He pushed open the door and gestured for me to walk inside. "I guess, maybe because of our size—physical size and population—it just seems a bit more personal here? I almost never hear or see anyone straight-up making fun of Kingsley and the way we live, but I often feel like the comments and laughter and pictures and posts are just one step shy of it. So, it often can feel like our little town is being made fun of without actually being made fun of." He scoffed. "That sounds ridiculous. I guess I'd never voiced those thoughts." He waved a hand as if dismissing the conversation. "We're grateful to the people who come to visit. They keep our town alive. We owe a lot to Ellie. Without her BnB, this town wouldn't survive."

I stood in the middle of what was most definitely a workshop and tried to pick my jaw up off the floor. I was surrounded by toolboxes and drills, sanders and saws—I recognized them from television and movies, not that I'd *ever* used any of the items.

But the part that had me in awe was the craftsmanship of Jordan's carpentry work. "You made all of this?" I asked in an impressed whisper as I moved slowly from piece to piece. My hand automatically wanted to feel the smooth wood, but I paused. "Can I touch?"

Jordan smiled, almost shyly. "Yes. Everything right now is raw or has already been stained, so it's safe."

My hand caressed the smooth wood grain of a rocking chair before I moved to a dresser, a corner cabinet, a chest, and finally a table. "Holy shit, you made all of this?" I repeated.

Jordan chuckled. "Yeah. That's only my second table and chairs set. I'd never done one of those, but Ellie convinced me to try. The one for her place turned out well, so I thought I'd try another. This year, Ellie has finally talked me into making my work available for custom order. So, she's going to mark the items at the BnB that I'd be able to make. And have a *catalog* of sorts of my other items. I seriously doubt anyone is going to actually order a table and chairs set, but they might be interested in some of the birdhouses or rocking chairs."

"That's an amazing idea. The rockers on her front porch and the back deck are made by you?"

Jordan nodded.

"And all the birdhouses?"

Another nod.

"What about the beds?"

He shook his head with a laugh. "Haven't gotten to that point yet. But you're definitely Ellie's grandson; she's been asking for me to make at least a couple beds."

"Every single item in this workshop should be in the catalog with base price and price levels for any customization. I guarantee that those same city visitors who take selfies with the chickens and the veggie stand cash bucket would think nothing of shelling out several thousand on custom-crafted, real-wood furniture and décor items." The excited thrill that always zinged through me with a sales project had me smiling from ear-to-ear. "You could make a killing."

Jordan shrugged. "I get by fine. If I end up too busy with bigger carpentry projects, then I lose time to tend the vegetables and chickens and take care of handyman jobs around town."

I pursed my lips. "Okay, I get that. But what about hiring on? If you could have help with the veggies and the chickens, maybe help with the fix-it-up projects in town, and help with the carpentry work, that would allow you to still *do* all of it the way you like—since you obviously enjoy it all—but you wouldn't be tied down to making sure it all got done on your own."

Jordan wrinkled his nose. "Like employees? I don't know. I like doing it all myself. I need to know it's done right."

"Hear me out—and this isn't an overnight thing—you

hire someone to help with the handyman services first. Then as you're able to bring in more money from the carpentry business, you hire someone to help with the chickens and veggies. One or two teens or even an older retiree. That gives you *more* time for the carpentry. Eventually, you can hire on an apprentice of sorts for the carpentry side of things." I was pacing around the workshop excitedly as the plans filled my head. "You wouldn't have to *give up* any of it, but you'd be able to slowly expand—with employees you trust—so that the carpentry—where you'd be able to make the most money —would be as productive as possible."

Jordan eyed me for a moment before smiling. "In theory, it sounds great. But there are a lot of holes. One, money. I have some savings, but I'm not sure I want to throw it at something that isn't assured. Two, there aren't a lot of people in Kingsley and even fewer who could do the carpentry or handyman work. Where would I find employees for that part? Pretty sure there aren't a lot of people trying to move to a town so small you'd miss it if you blinked just to do odd jobs or build rocking chairs."

I cocked my head to the side. "*You're* here. You love it. Out of all the people in the world, I'm a thousand percent sure there are people who would fight for the chance to move here and live a simple, happy life doing something they love."

"But not you," Jordan quipped.

I smirked. "Not me. Definitely *not* a handyman or carpenter."

"Why *are* you here?" Jordan asked.

"Ellie didn't tell you all about her overworked grandson?"

He shook his head.

I wasn't giving up on the business expansion plan, but I took the distraction. "Been having tons of headaches. Exhausted, anxious, loss of appetite, not sleeping well. I finally gave in and went to the doctor thinking he'd throw some pills at me. No such luck." I chuckled without humor. "His prescription was two months off work. Like completely off work."

"And you just up and left work for two months?" Jordan cocked his head.

"Well, I likely wouldn't have, but my grandparents and father heard the doctor reiterating his advice. Plus, they are all close. Doc Barret likely would have spilled to at least Gran or Gramps—maybe not a full-on diagnosis, but his concern." I shrugged. "Honestly, I hate the idea of being away from my work. *But* when the medical professional says you're working your way into an early grave, it kinda messes with your head. I knew I was dealing with a lot of stress and anxiety. Maybe a break will get me back on track."

"So, two months away will magically make the stress of your city job go away?" Jordan asked.

"Well, my banishment ended up being *three* months. And, no. I don't think the stress of work will be gone. Maybe I'll just be more rested and better able to deal with it? Despite being woken up at the ass-crack of dawn by a *rude* rooster," I teased, "I slept well last night and don't have my usual pounding headache."

"That sounds promising," Jordan said. "And I'd like to say the early wake-up was a fluke, but Hank *is* rude and he'll crow until he thinks everyone is up." He paused and frowned. "How did two go to three?"

"Well, my sister messed up something on one of the sales accounts. Since I was already leaving, I took the blame thinking I'd save her being in the doghouse."

"Nice brother."

I smirked. "Yeah, well, throwing myself under the bus to save her really backfired. Gramps decided the mistake—the one I didn't even make—was worthy of an extra month of rest and relaxation."

"Ouch." Jordan smiled softly. "So, how did Kingsley become your destination?"

"Gramps and Gran kinda insisted."

"And you didn't fight it?"

"Nah. I love Gran and Gramps. They're more parents to me than my actual father. I haven't seen my mother since I was young. I hear from her every year or so. She's out in Hollywood trying to make it big." I glanced around the workshop. "Spending three months out of work is a nightmare, but being with Gran makes it a bit easier."

"You've never been to Kingsley to visit? I know I've seen your sister at Ellie's."

"No, for a while, it was because I was so busy—Dad kept me super busy with sports and social activities. Then it was just because I didn't want to or I had school or work." I shrugged.

"But not Marissa?"

"No, she was *normal* so Dad left her alone."

Jordan gave a sad smile. "I wonder what it would be like to feel or be normal."

I took a step closer. "Boring. Normal is overrated. There's not a thing wrong with you or me. We're who we are. Fuck anyone who doesn't like it."

"I think I could have used that attitude when I was teenager. I fought being gay for so long. Wasn't until I was in my early twenties that I actually accepted it."

"And you don't want to date or settle down?" I asked softly. Why was I moving even closer to Jordan? As magical as his *mouth* was, I was quickly figuring out that his whole person had some sort of weird draw on me.

"*Wanting* isn't the problem. I do want that. It's just not something available here. And I love my life here too much to leave. So, I make do." A flash of sadness crossed his face.

One more step and I'd be close enough to touch him. The air was thick with the scent of wood and varnish. Sexual tension surrounded us and my heart thumped in my chest. Last night was in the past. That was where it would have remained if Jordan had been any other sexual encounter. That was where it *should* have remained. But my lips tingled at the memory of the kisses we'd shared. My dick twitched as I recalled his lips wrapped around me. "We have three months to *make do*," I whispered as I stepped close enough to press into Jordan's personal space and back him against the workbench.

He swallowed so hard I heard it and I leaned in to kiss at his bobbing Adam's apple.

"Not sure that's a good idea," Jordan answered, but his head fell back to allow me better access to his neck.

"Why's that?" I asked. Flirting was something that came naturally for me, but this flirting was hiding the alarm bells in my head that told me to step away and keep things platonic from here on out.

"You're my best friend's grandson."

I nibbled at his jaw. "Gran knows I'm gay. She knows you're gay. I doubt she'd be offended or even surprised."

"I have work to do to help Ellie get ready for the season," Jordan said breathlessly.

My lips moved against the shell of his ear. "I'm here to help." I almost laughed. As if *me* being there to help was going to be a big benefit as far as labor.

"You're a terrible dresser," Jordan choked out words on what sounded like a moan.

I gasped. "*That* is offensive and totally unfair. I have yet to go shopping for my country boy clothes."

He smiled, the action bringing out the crinkles around his eyes that I was beginning to adore.

Warning! *Warning*! Never start anything sexual with a man who you're beginning to adore. It's like rule number one of random and meaningless hookups.

Jordan closed the distance between our mouths and devoured my lips. I opened to welcome his probing and teasing tongue inside. Immediately, my body was on fire for his touch, as if the magic of his mouth had set me aflame.

All too soon, he pulled away and closed his eyes as if trying to compose himself.

"You can't tell me you wouldn't like to do that for three months," I murmured as I ran a hand through his thick brown hair and settled it at the nape of his neck.

"The issue isn't *not* enjoying that for three months," Jordan said slowly. "The issue is enjoying it so much that I'd be wrecked when you left. I'm a romantic, Oxford," He gave a somewhat defeated wink as if he'd already resigned himself to turning down whatever we could possibly enjoy during my time in Kingsley. "I get that you do random hookups with no intentions of dating or settling down."

"You said you do the same," I accused, feeling desperate to get him to agree to a three-month fling.

"I do random hookups that don't lead anywhere because of my life, my job, this town. It's not that I don't want to date and settle down. I *do*. You're the type of guy I could totally fall for—which is totally strange because I've never had a thing for city boys, but there's definitely a draw." He licked his lips, his eyes traveling from my mouth to my eyes and back as if he was struggling not to kiss me again. "And where does that leave me in three months? You're back in the city and I'm here nursing a broken heart while being reminded of all that I'll never have. As much as I *want* to make the most of your time here, I feel like keeping my distance is the smartest thing for me."

I pursed my lips into a pout but nodded. "I get that. I do. I have to tell you, as much as I think we could have an explosive three months, I definitely think I'd go back to the city with a bit of a chip in my heart at least. I truly have *never* felt as drawn to someone as I do to you." I brushed a thumb over his lips. "But I can respect your decision and even appreciate that you're trying to protect us both." I leaned in a feather a kiss at the corner of his mouth. "Just know that I'll accept a change of mind if you decide to risk it."

FOUR

JORDAN

I GROANED as I rolled from bed even before Hank's wake-up call. I'd slept like shit and needed copious amounts of coffee to get my day started.

Marc was coming over to help with chores and then we were heading to a nearby store where he could buy some work clothes. *Nearby* meant a forty-five-minute drive. Figured we'd get there at the store's opening time, do shopping, grab lunch, and then get back in time for at least a few small jobs and then evening chores. I didn't want to ask Ellie or any of the townspeople to cover the evening chores; I did that a couple times a year when I went to the bigger towns and even that felt like too much.

As I boiled water and automatically set up two cups of coffee—Marc swore he'd be over early—I let my mind drift.

To the night at the bar.

Taking Marc to the river bluff.

The sparks that flew between us.

How I'd felt elated and dismayed all at once when I realized he was here in Kingsley for three months.

All of the reasons I had absolutely no business wanting

anything to happen between us.

My dick twitched as if to say *What reasons, damn it?*

"Oh, let's see," I mumbled to myself as I scooped coffee into the filters. "First, he's only here for a short time. Second, he's a lot younger than me. Third, he's Ellie's grandson. Fourth, he's a city slicker through-and-through." I poured the water over the coffee and breathed deeply as the scent of the brew filled the air. "Did I mention that he's only here for a short time?"

I knew myself. Knew that if I let myself get involved with him—no matter how often I reminded myself it was just sex and he was leaving—I'd fall hard. And then I'd be wrecked when he left.

But what are the three months going to be like? Can you be around him, working with him daily, getting to know him, and not be wrecked just the same? If you're going to be wrecked either way, why not add amazing sex to the mix?

My head and dick had good arguments.

But my heart was thumping with warnings. *Don't get involved. Sex makes everything more intimate and emotional. It will be hard enough to be around him and not touch him—even harder when he leaves—but adding sex to the situation will come back to slap you in the face when you're inevitably alone and miserable over what you want but can't have. Will never have.*

I growled and pulled breakfast sandwiches out of the fridge. Ellie had sent a huge lunch the day before and included the biscuits stuffed full of eggs, bacon, and cheese. I wrapped them in a paper towel and warmed them up in the microwave.

A knock at the door pulled me from my head. "Come in," I called out.

Marc came through the door, hair somewhat less-than-perfect, sleepy eyes that sent a zing through my blood, and a soft smile. "Am I late? I got up with Hank's first outburst."

I chuckled. "You're fine." I glanced up and down his body. "Same clothes from yesterday?"

He shrugged. "I didn't want to ruin any of my other stuff."

I cocked my head to the side. "You wanna wear some of my things? May feel a bit better to be in work clothes when we go shopping."

"What? You mean instead of my perfectly mismatched fashion disaster?" Marc held a hand to his chest in mock offense.

I laughed. "You look uniquely adorable, but I've got some jeans you can wear. They might be *slightly* big, but I've got a belt."

"I'd be happy to try your stuff on." He glanced at his feet. "The shoes are the issue though."

"You can borrow a pair of boots."

Marc's eyes sparkled as he stepped closer. "I've seen your...*hands*...among other things. What makes you think your big-ass boots would fit me?"

I threw my head back and laughed before decreasing the space between us even more. *What the fuck I was doing*? "Don't forget. I've seen your...*hands*...among other things," I mimicked. "I think my boots will come very close to fitting."

Marc stared at my lips for a moment before leaning in and brushing a kiss over my cheek. "I'd very much like to start this day and the next eighty-eight with your tongue down my throat. Any chance you've reconsidered?"

I swallowed thickly and took a deep breath. With a chaste kiss against his cheek, I shook my head and stepped away.

Marc's face fell and he hung his head. "I don't know that I've ever hated a rejection so badly."

"Like you've ever been rejected," I scoffed.

"Okay, point. But it doesn't make it any easier."

"I'm sorry. I'm definitely torn. My head and my dick *want*

more than anything to say yes. My heart is screaming at me that I need to protect myself." Without thinking—and simply because it felt right—I reached out and wrapped Marc in my arms. As I hugged him close, I felt my heart sink to the floor. There was absolutely no way I was going to be able to avoid this man for eighty-eight more days.

He fit against me so perfectly—as if my soul sighed in relief at finally finding its home. I mentally chastised myself for thinking that. *See? That right there—those thoughts and feelings—that's the exact reason why I have absolutely no reason getting involved with Marcus Kingsley.*

Marcus nuzzled his face against my neck. "Look, I'll respect whatever decision you make. I'll even agree that us keeping things platonic is probably the smartest choice in the long run." He brushed a kiss along the sensitive skin of my throat. "And I've always figured myself for a pretty smart guy," he said with a smile in his voice, "but there's a part of me that very much wants to strongly suggest we enjoy this time we've been given."

I chuckled into the top of his head. "Would that be the part that's currently pressing against my hip?" God, how I wanted to drop to my knees for this man.

Marc laughed. "Perhaps." He pulled away slightly and leaned into me, his forehead resting against mine. "Maybe *knowing* there's a definite end date would make it easier? We wouldn't be starting a relationship and then thinking all was fine and dandy only to have it ripped away in an unexpected break-up. We'd *know* it was temporary." He sighed. "I'm not going to badger you into something you don't want to do. But at the risk of sounding like a broken record, I'm on board if you change your mind."

I continued to hold him in my arms for much longer than was necessary or smart before releasing him with a deep breath. "Well, let's get you into some jeans and boots. The flannel shirt should be just fine. It doesn't even look like you got a speck of dirt on it yesterday," I teased.

"I'll have you know, I cleaned tons of mud from my shoes. The hems of these pants are ruined. And there was some sort of dried something from the veggies on my shirt when I put it on this morning," Marc feigned indignation.

He followed me to my bedroom and it wasn't lost on me that we were both very aware of my king-sized bed and all of the fun we could have in it. *Do it. Chuck the plans. Take him to bed. The shopping can wait.*

"No," I muttered.

"What?" Marc asked.

"Oh, nothing. Just talking to myself. Not used to having anyone but the chickens around most of the time." I pulled out a worn pair of jeans that were probably my slimmest fitting ones. "These should be fine in length and I'll grab a belt. You can use the bathroom to change if you want."

Marc's eyes were a mixture of fire and mischief as he undid the button of his dress pants. "You've had my cock in your mouth," he said gruffly as he let the material fall to his ankles to reveal a mouth-watering bulge under a pair of perfectly-fitting boxer briefs. "Pretty sure seeing me without pants isn't considered inappropriate after the river."

I swallowed thickly with a nod. "Probably not." I handed him the jeans.

He never took his eyes from mine as he unfolded the denim, stepped into them, and pulled them up over his strong, lean thighs. Marc turned to look in the mirror as he buttoned the waist. "These are *definitely* not my designer brand and they don't do much for my ass, but they're a shit-ton better than picking veggies, gathering eggs, and building furniture in slacks."

I laughed. "I'd beg to differ about what they do for your ass, Oxford," I said before my head to mouth filter could kick in. I cleared my throat. "If you had jeans at home, why not bring those?" I handed him a belt.

Marc smirked at my slip of tongue, but gave me a look of shock as he put a hand to his chest. "What? Wear my custom designer jeans to work on a farm? Well, I *never*."

"Did the jeans cost even more than the dress pants?" I was truly in the dark when it came to fashion. I had a few pairs of boots—most for work, some for nicer events—quite a few pairs of work jeans—some in better shape than others —and a multitude of t-shirts and flannel button-ups. Aside from the addition of winter coats, coveralls, and gloves, I really didn't have need for much more.

"The jeans definitely cost more. They were custom made for me. I may be a fashion whore in a lot of ways, but I don't have my dress pants custom made. So, they are much easier to replace. Same with the Oxfords."

"If you say so," I teased. "Let's get boots and breakfast before we head out."

Two hours later, we'd gathered eggs, checked on the chickens, picked veggies and put them at the roadside stand, and carried a delivery of lumber from the driveway to the workshop.

"I don't suppose a nap is part of the plan?" Marc grumbled as we headed toward my truck.

"No, but we can stop for *fancy* coffee on the way. And after shopping, we'll get lunch." I smiled and started the engine.

"All before we come back here to do it all again, right?"

I nodded. "A country boy's work is never done."

Marc groaned. "*This* was not what I had in mind when the doctor said I needed a break from work." He flopped his head against the seat and rolled it to look at me. "But tell me more about this fancy coffee."

Forty-five minutes later, we were armed with the fanciest

coffee the area had to offer as we walked into the farm and tractor supply store.

"Wow," Marc hummed as he sipped his coffee. "The sign indicated farm and tractor supplies, but this place is huge."

"Yeah, it's got pretty much anything a farmer could need." I headed toward the men's clothing section.

Marc caught up with me. "Do I smell popcorn?"

I laughed. "Yeah, you want some? They always have popcorn available."

He licked his lips. "That actually sounds delish, but I better not since I'm trying on clothes. Don't want to get butter stains on the pants."

A few minutes later, we stood in the middle of the clothing section and Marc's jaw was on the floor while his nose was wrinkled as if he'd seen something foul.

"I know it's not the upscale stores you're used to, but you just need some work pants. Jeans are likely the best. I mean, we could maybe go for Carhartt pants, but we'd need to special order those." I wasn't exactly defensive, but I definitely felt the need to soothe Marc's senses.

"No, these are fine," he answered absently.

"Why do you look disgusted?"

He shook his head. "It's not disgust." Then his eyes met mine. "Okay, the camo is definitely gross. I never knew there were so many forms of camo."

I laughed. "Yeah, camo is a staple around these parts."

"I guess I never knew Wrangler had so many different styles; to be honest, I really wasn't even aware Wrangler was a real brand. I think I thought it was like a fictional brand on cowboy movies or something." Marc scanned the rows of folded jeans. "And does this place sell only Wrangler?"

I chuckled. "Yeah, it's their top seller, so they stock it exclusively. They carry the top fifty most popular cuts and designs in almost every denim wash. They can order the others. They also sell other brands, but it's on order only."

Marc looked at the images above the shelves of jeans. "*Those* are *not* the Wranglers I've always pictured in my mind on movie cowboys. Those almost look good."

I snorted. "They do. Let's get you in a few pairs. We still need to get you some boots."

Thirty minutes later, I was convinced that shopping for jeans with Marc was the best and worst thing in the world. He wanted to show me every pair he tried on—and that included making me determine which ones made his ass look the best.

"You're going to be working on a farm. Who's going to see your ass?" I grumbled as I adjusted my thickening cock after he'd shown me a particularly sexy pair. "But add those to the purchase pile. They were probably the best. Just make sure they are comfortable enough to actually *work* in."

Marc popped his head out of the curtained fitting room and smiled seductively. "You never know. Maybe some sexy guy on that farm will see my ass in these jeans, throw caution to the wind, and spend three months fucking me." He winked.

I scoffed to cover my groan and tried to think of *anything* aside from how badly I wanted what he described.

"Never underestimate the power of a great fitting pair of jeans," Marc called from behind the curtain. "Can you get me a few shirts to try on? I figure I'll find a couple I like and get several in different colors. I'm not as concerned about the shirts."

"You're determined to get the *just right* jeans, but the shirts are no big deal?" I teased, but walked away to grab some shirts.

When I returned, Marc smiled. "I can make almost *any* shirt look amazing. But even *this* ass needs jeans that are at least a flattering cut." He turned away from me and slapped a hand on his perfect ass.

I rolled my eyes. "Did the doctor mention your lack of confidence? I'm worried you don't see yourself in a very positive light."

Marc cackled as he stepped out in one of the shirts. "I may come across confident—and don't get me wrong, I *am* in a lot of areas—but there are definitely some points in my life where I doubt my every move."

I cocked a brow.

Marc just shook his head. "Never mind. That's more than I want to get into on a shopping trip." He gathered three pairs of jeans and five shirts. "If you'll let me keep your pair, that should be plenty of jeans." He wrinkled his nose. "They may not be custom designer jeans, but they aren't cheap. Kinda hate to spend *too* much for clothes I won't wear after three months."

I nodded and pushed away the feeling of being punched in the gut. Despite *knowing* he was only here for a short time, I had a hard time not letting my head and heart picture him as a permanent fixture in my life.

Oh, he's a permanent fixture. I huffed at the thought. *Don't act like he won't be in your head and heart from here on out despite the fact that he's going to hightail it back to the city. You know you'll never forget him—intimate relationship or not. Your sorry ass will wallow in the what-could-have-been and what-I'll-never-have cesspool of loneliness for years to come thanks to this guy.*

My thoughts were way too accurate, so I cleared my throat. "Maybe you'll bring Wranglers to the city and be the next trendsetter," I joked as I grabbed an abandoned cart from the middle of the aisle. "Throw them in here. Boots next."

Boots were easier. Marc quickly found a style he liked, decided he needed two pairs, and we headed to the checkout.

"You want that popcorn?" I asked as we neared the machine producing the salty, buttery goodness.

"Are we going straight to lunch?" Marc asked.

I nodded. "Yeah, probably. Not a whole lot more to do." I glanced at my phone. "Well, it will be more like *brunch*."

Marc's eyes went wide and he snorted when he saw the time. "I guess getting up at Hank's ass-crack of dawn will do that to a person. Let's share a popcorn, you show me around town a bit, and then lunch."

We got a bag of popcorn, I tossed in some donation money, and we continued toward the checkout.

"They don't even charge for the popcorn?" Marc exclaimed in a hushed whisper. "You country people kill me," he bumped his hip against mine.

He didn't even flinch when the fairly high total flashed on the register. I'd figured he was well-off because I knew Ellie's family was pretty much *rich* by most standards. I could have paid the amount without hurting my checking account— although, I likely would have spread the purchases out over a month or so. Despite money not being all that important to me—okay, yes, money was important so I could survive; I just never based everything on money—it made me feel better to know that I wasn't just a *poor* country boy compared to the rich city boy. My money in the city was likely *nothing*, but at least I held my own in and around Kingsley.

Why did that even matter to me? I scowled at my thoughts.

Probably because you're preparing for when he leaves and knowing that he didn't leave because you're a poor country boy is at least something.

I wasn't sure if that made complete sense, but I was sick of thinking of him leaving, so I pushed the thought away.

We spent about an hour driving around the town. It was still *small* compared to Rockhurst, but it was a lot bigger than

Kingsley. This town had a stoplight; Kingsley did not. This town had four restaurants compared to Kingsley's two—not counting Ellie's place, but she only cooked for guests.

"I'll let you decide, but my suggestion for lunch is the Candle Light Diner."

Marc raised a brow. "Sounds romantic. What are the other choices?"

"A fish place that I swear once gave me food poisoning so I avoid it. A Chinese place that is usually pretty tasty. And a pizza place. Candle Light has the best food of all four."

"Better than Gran's?" Marc smirked.

"Nothing is better than Ellie's cooking."

"Okay, Candle Light Diner it is then."

I parked the truck and we headed toward the door. Once seated, I suddenly felt nervous.

"I know this isn't the glamourous sushi, escargot, and caviar you're probably used to, but they make some really good food."

Marc laughed. "While I *love* sushi and will be *dying* for some by the time I go home, I'm *not* a fan of escargot or caviar. Just because I'm from the city doesn't mean I only eat fancy food." He opened the menu just as I ordered tea to drink. Marc nodded politely. "Same, please."

I feigned shock. "I don't know if I can be friends with someone who likes sushi."

"What?! It's soooo good," Marc exclaimed. "Now, I will admit that I usually only like the cooked kind so a lot of people would say I'm not a true sushi enthusiast."

My brows shot up. "There's *cooked* sushi? Why did I think all sushi is raw?"

The waitperson brought our drinks and offered to give us a few more minutes to decide.

"A lot of people think that. I did until a friend took me and showed me what to order. Maybe you can come to the

city sometime and I'll introduce you to the joys of sushi."
Something flashed across Marc's face, but it was gone before
I could analyze it.

"I don't see that ever happening," I said.

Before I could decide if I meant the city or the sushi or
both, Marc coughed and sputtered and looked at the glass of
tea as if it had greatly offended him. "What the actual hell is
that?" he demanded in a harsh whisper.

I frowned. "Tea?"

"*That* is not tea. They've accidentally put syrup in the
glass or something. Oh my God, that's terrible. It's like
pouring sugar water on my tongue."

After a sip of what tasted like perfectly good iced tea, I
chuckled. "I take it you're not a fan of sweet tea?"

Marc grimaced. "Sweet tea is fine. Like a bit of sugar to
take the edge off or a couple packets of Splenda or whatever
—I actually prefer stevia, but that's not the point—but *that* is
just wrong. Why don't you just inject sugar right into your
veins?" He stuck a spoon in the glass and stirred. "I think it's
actually thicker than regular tea because of the sugar. This
should be a crime."

I rolled my eyes. "Oh my God, Oxford, get over it. Order a
water, I'll drink your tea." I nudged his menu. "Figure out
what you want to eat."

Marc moved the offending glass of sweet tea toward me
and picked up the menu.

I already knew what I wanted, so I took the time to enjoy
my tea and watch him as he read the items on the menu.
After a few moments, his eyes went wide.

"What's *bread and gravy*?" he asked.

"Just what it sounds like. Soft, chewy chunks of bread
covered in white ham gravy. Kinda like biscuits and gravy, but
with ham and bread instead of sausage and biscuits."

Marc wrinkled his nose. "So, it's basically pouring liquid fat on carbohydrate pieces and calling it a meal?"

I laughed. "Pretty much. It's really good. But I'm going to suggest you get something else here—their bread and gravy is good, but Ellie's is a thousand times better."

He gave me a look that said he didn't believe me. "I'm glad Gran saves her country cooking for Kingsley or Gramps. I don't know what eating bread and gravy would have done to my childhood."

"That's it. I'm definitely having Ellie fix it. And I want to be there when you take your first bite and almost orgasm over how good it is."

The mention of orgasm brought the night at the river flooding back and I immediately regretted the words.

Marc smirked and winked. "I think that's a challenge I'm going to have to accept."

He ended up ordering a tenderloin sandwich with onion rings—and laughing his ass off when the tenderloin ended up as big as his head; the man seriously took a picture of the breaded pork next to his noggin as proof.

I ordered the meatloaf and mashed potatoes.

He took the homemade roll I offered from my plate, and I couldn't help but laugh at how much he liked it. "You better let Ellie make some of those, too."

Marc was curious about sugar cream pie, but I convinced him to try Ellie's first.

"Seriously, this place has good everything, but Ellie's is always better."

"I can't believe she can cook all this stuff and never had me try it."

"I think she makes all this stuff a lot, maybe you just weren't ever around to try it."

Marc's face fell for a moment, but he returned to eating his sandwich.

The drive back to Kingsley was quiet and gave me way too much time to think.

Marc fell asleep, his head lolling forward a few times before his body slanted toward mine and he rested against my shoulder.

My chest ached. I would have given anything to have a man I cared for by my side, working with me, enjoying a day of shopping and lunch. Marc could be that man. There'd never been these feelings toward a random hook-up before.

That's because he's much more than a random hook-up.

I sighed.

Yeah, he's my best friend's grandson which means too young and too off-limits.

Do you really think the age difference is that big of a deal?

I shrugged internally. It was ten years and that didn't mean anything at our age. At eighteen and eight or twenty-five and fifteen? Yeah, definite issue. But at thirty and forty it was nothing but an excuse.

And what makes you think Ellie would be anything less than thrilled to see you and Marc together and happy?

I smiled at the thought of my best friend. I knew she'd love to see me happy and if it also brought Marc happiness she'd be over-the-moon.

But the issue wasn't really about age or being off-limits.

The issue was Marc was temporary.

Marc couldn't wait to get back to the city.

To his job.

To his real life.

Kingsley was just a blip. Just a moment in time for him to catch his breath and recharge. I couldn't expect him to give up his life and live in Kingsley for me. Just as he'd never dream of asking me to move to Rockhurst.

Who's talking about moving and forever? It's three months of hot sex. Nothing more, nothing less. At best, you see him a couple times a year to burn up the sheets.

And at worst? I thought with a grimace.

At worst, you don't see him again, but you have three months of time to cherish forever.

"And a broken heart to nurse," I mumbled.

'Tis better to have loved and lost, than never to have loved at all.

I scoffed quietly. "Okay, Lord Tennyson." I shook my head as I pulled onto the gravel road that led to my property. "Doesn't make the loss part any easier," I whispered so low even I could barely hear it.

This situation seemed to come from nowhere. It wasn't planned. It's filled with possibility and potential. Maybe it's fate and you should take what it's handing you.

"Possibility and potential to fail and be an epic disaster," I grumbled softly. Would it have been best if I'd never seen Marc at the Shilesville bar? Never had that night with him by the river?

I glanced down at his perfectly mussed dark-blond hair, the dark lashes feathering his cheeks, the pink lips that I knew could light me on fire. No, being with him was something I'd never want to miss out on.

Then why are you pushing away the chance to spend three months with him?

"Because I can already feel the hurt of losing him and it scares the hell out of me," I whispered. Knowing that Marc would easily walk away and return to his regularly scheduled life while leaving me to pick up the pieces was killing me.

Marc snored and shifted on my shoulder.

So, because of fear, you're going to live to regret the time you didn't spend with him just so you can protect your heart?

I huffed. Was I wrong to want to avoid hurt?

Life is full of hurts. Think of all you'd miss out on if you skipped it because you might get hurt.

"Might is the wrong word in this situation," I muttered. "I *will* get hurt. Definitely." My heart tugged in my chest, pulling so strongly toward the man asleep on my shoulder it was almost painful. Maybe what we could have together—even if for such a short time—was worth the pain.

I pulled into the driveway and put the truck in *park*.

If he was here indefinitely, what would you do?

Easy. I'd have him in my bed, in my life, in a heartbeat.

Then why let something like a time limit stop you? None of us are guaranteed a certain amount of time.

I sighed. If Marc wasn't interested, I would have likely left well-enough alone.

Instead, I pushed the fear of heartache away, shifted in my seat, and cupped Marc's stubble-roughened cheek in my hand. "Hey, Oxford. We're home."

His eyes fluttered open and he blinked several times before his whole face relaxed and he leaned into my hand. "I could get used to you waking me up," he whispered.

"I could get used to waking you up." I slowly closed the distance between us until my mouth was just a breath away from his.

"Did we drive through a portal?" Marc smiled sleepily. "When I fell asleep, you were determined to keep things platonic. Now, you're looking very much like you might want to kiss me."

I smiled. "*Wanting* to kiss you has never been the problem."

Marc licked his lips.

"Can I?" I asked gruffly.

He smirked. "Can you what?"

"Kiss you."

"I've wanted you to kiss me every moment since the river," Marc murmured.

My lips captured his. I caught his gasp with my mouth

and dipped my tongue in to dance with his. My body immediately caught fire as the kiss deepened.

Kissing had always been enjoyable.

Kissing Marc was so far beyond enjoyable—the heat, the electricity, the passion, and the power—I wanted to bottle it up and use it to run the world.

When we broke apart several moments later, Marc rested his forehead against mine. "At the risk of breaking the spell or waking up from a really great dream, what changed?"

I brushed a kiss over his lips and shook my head. "It's going to hurt, but life is full of hurts. As much as I'll hate myself in three months, I can't spend this time miserable and fighting to keep my hands off you. You're like a magnet, drawing me in, and I want whatever we can have for however long we can have it."

Marc's eyes sparkled and he wrapped his arms around my neck and kissed me long and deep. "I'm not down for the heartache, but I'm one hundred percent on board with the rest."

I shifted to pull him onto my lap, but his hip hit the horn and the sound blasted through the air. "Well, that was a mood-killer," I grumbled.

Marc laughed. "Nah, just a time-out. I *do* think we should have a level-headed, non-sex-fueled conversation about parameters and such." He kissed me. "Maybe we finish those chores and talk over dinner?"

"Perfect. First thing I want to do is show you how big that zucchini is."

Marc busted out laughing. "Is that a veggie farmer pick-up line?"

I snorted. "Guess you'll have to find out."

We climbed from the truck and headed toward the house. It would hurt later, but for the time being, my heart was full and I knew I'd made the best decision of my life.

FIVE
MARC

"OH MY GOD, IT'S HUGE!"

Jordan laughed. "That's what all the boys say."

"I bet," I teased. "For real, it was thinner and shorter than my forearm yesterday and now it's the size of my entire arm."

"Yeah, it would have been a perfect pick yesterday, but I left it to show you what happens." Jordan hefted the enormous squash from under its leafy hiding place and twisted it from the vine. "This one is no good for anything but zucchini bread now."

My nose wrinkled. "You put zucchini in your bread?"

"It's good. Kinda sweet. It's the consistency of banana bread. Ellie makes it for her guests and always has some loaves ready to sell. She sells out daily."

"I'll take your word for it."

We gathered the rest of the vegetables and Jordan texted the grocer, Sandy.

"I'll leave the basket on the porch. If she wants to pick them up this evening, she can. If not, I'll add them to the morning's haul and drop them off." Jordan hefted the basket of produce on his hip. "Eggs are next. Go ahead and go grab the baskets. I'll meet you at the chicken coop."

I headed toward the coop and picked up the wire baskets Jordan had shown me the day before. Hank the rooster was in another area of the yard and Jordan promised he mostly stayed away when humans were around. The hens came scurrying over to see if I brought food. "Sorry, ladies. Maybe Jordan has some treats. I'm just here to help gather the fruits of your labor." I snorted.

"What are you laughing about?" Jordan asked as he came up from behind and stood close enough I could feel his heat.

When his lips teased along my neck, I dropped my head back. "No more laughing. The situation just went from funny to sexy. Is it considered a kink to be turned on in a chicken coop?"

Jordan laughed. "Only if the chickens or rooster are the ones turning you on."

"No, definitely not them. It's their damn sexy farmer who has me all hot and bothered." I pressed my ass against Jordan's groin and moaned as his lips continued to kiss the skin from my neck to my jaw.

"Let's get these eggs and clean the coop. We can continue this later."

I groaned and handed him a basket. "You're a cock tease," I joked. "Get it? Since we're on a farm with a rooster? Cock?"

Jordan rolled his eyes. "Yeah, I get it."

"I was laughing at the idea of eggs being hen fruit. Earlier I mean," I explained. "The girls were excited like they thought I brought food and I told them I was just here to gather the fruits of their labor. It made me laugh."

A look I couldn't quite place flashed over Jordan's face, but it was gone before I could analyze it. Then he snickered. "You're a real comedian, huh?" He walked into the area where the nests were located. "Okay, any cracked ones put in the spare basket. We can't use those. If they are super dirty, they go in this basket." He held up a wire container. "If no cracks and no dirt, put them in your own basket."

Since the chickens had returned to their foraging for food, I had no issues collecting the eggs. If they'd been *on* the nests? Oh, hell no; I wasn't reaching under a chicken's nether regions to grab her egg.

I put a cracked egg in the throw away basket. Then three went in the dirty basket. And I ended up with five in my basket. "Do you just let them soak to clean them?"

"No, never let eggs soak. That allows bacteria inside. We'll scrub gently with an unscented soap and dry with disposable towels. The scrub brush has to be bleached after to keep from spreading bacteria."

"Eeww, I'm glad I get my eggs from the store. Fresh eggs sound disgusting."

Jordan stared at me for a moment and then narrowed his eyes. "Where do you think the eggs you buy in the store come from?"

I shrugged. "I mean, chickens, of course. But not like dirty farm chickens. I prefer my eggs clean and cold."

Jordan rolled his eyes. "Hate to break it to you, but store eggs are likely coming from settings that are much dirtier than this and the chickens are very likely not treated well at all. Big producers care only about production, not about the health and well-being of their animals or the eggs."

"Oh, I didn't know that." I pursed my lips. "Still, I want my eggs clean and cold."

"Did you know most Europeans don't refrigerate their farm-fresh eggs? Honestly, eggs fresh from the nest and into food are the very best and most delicious. We won't wash the eggs that are already clean. They have a coating on them called the *bloom* that protects the porous surface from bacteria getting in. They don't have to be refrigerated. The ones we have to wash will need to be because we'll remove the bloom." Jordan checked the remaining nests and gathered up the various baskets. "Never use an egg that has been previously refrigerated and then left out to warm. Bacteria can start to grow."

"So, are you telling me that you, Gran, and most of Kingsley use farm-fresh eggs?" I grimaced. "It's probably just something in my head, but I'm pretty sure I'll never be able to eat the kind straight from a chicken. Give me the store-bought kind any day."

Jordan shook his head. "You'd be surprised how much better the fresh ones taste. The ones from the store are far inferior."

"You keep your fresh ones."

"We'll see." Jordan smirked.

My phone buzzed as we walked toward the house.

Gran: *I planned on going back to Rockhurst for a day or so to see Gramps. A guy's car broke down in town and he needs a room. Could you keep an eye on the place? He's in the smallest room at the farthest end of the house. He knows there will be no breakfast for him other than just some cereal or the like. He's already paid. He plans to leave tomorrow if the shop can get his car fixed.*

My heart sank. Damn it. I couldn't tell Gran no, but I'd been looking forward to a night with Jordan.

"What's wrong?" he asked.

I explained the situation.

"That's not a problem. I know which room she's talking about. We'll hang out at the BnB instead of here. We can have our chat and whatever else over there just as easily as at my place."

"You don't care that someone might see you with me?" I cocked a brow.

Jordan frowned. "Weird that it hadn't even crossed my mind, but no. Plus, the guy is a stranger from out of town.

We'll let him know that he has the run of the television, kitchen, and the hallway bathroom. We'll be upstairs in *our quarters* if he needs us. He doesn't have to know that our quarters consist of your room."

"Sounds perfect. But I gotta say it's weird to think of some stranger in the house. Especially if our chat goes the way I plan for it to go." I waggled my brows.

"Your room is far from his. He won't have any idea what's going on as long as you can stay mostly quiet."

I shrugged. "No promises, but he's leaving tomorrow anyway."

I texted Gran to let her know I'd help her out no problem. I left out the part about Jordan coming over. I figured that was up to Jordan if and when he decided to tell Gran about us.

Whatever *us* ended up being.

∽

A BIT LATER, after we'd washed the eggs and our hands, cleaned up, and finished a couple odds and ends at Jordan's place, we drove separately over to Gran's.

It may or may not have been coincidence that Jordan hadn't deemed us ready to leave until he'd made a comment about seeing Gran make her exit. "Looks like Ellie's heading out," he'd mentioned as he nodded his chin toward the plume of dust down the road.

I didn't mind keeping our three-month fling a secret from Gran if that was how Jordan wanted to keep it. After all, I got to go back to Rockhurst. He was the one stuck here day in and day out with his best friend who happened to be my grandmother. Gran was pretty open-minded, but I didn't know how she'd react to the thought of her best friend fucking her grandson into the mattress.

And *that* was exactly what I planned on Jordan doing.

Or, I could fuck *him* into the mattress for the next three months.

Either way, I was fine with Gran not knowing about my sex life with her best friend if that was how Jordan wanted it to play out.

Once we'd pulled our vehicles around the side of Gran's barn where the non-guests parked, I smiled as I watched Jordan climb from his truck. He was the epitome of sex on legs and I licked my lips as I thought of all the fun we were going to have.

Only a very tiny part of me felt bad that he openly admitted he'd be crushed when I left. I knew without a doubt —based on how much I'd already started to enjoy my time with him—that I'd miss him when I left. But I had to be honest and say I was glad he'd opted to let this thing between us play out.

"Like what you see?" Jordan growled as he wrapped an arm around my waist and shoved me against the side of the barn. I love the way we'd immediately been able to go from attracted to each other, but holding back, to attracted to each other and acting on it with very little awkwardness or uncertainty.

The way my body ignited at Jordan's touch was a new sensation for me. With other men, I'd get turned on, but with Jordan it was as if my entire body was engulfed in flames of desire, and all he had to do was nuzzle my neck or press his body against mine. I had a feeling I'd simultaneously melt and explode when he had me naked and under him.

Or over him.

On him.

In him.

However he wanted me; I was open to several prepositions as they related to our upcoming sexual relationship.

"I very much like what I see," I murmured and pretended that it wasn't me who whimpered as my head fell back and his teeth nibbled at the skin between my neck and shoulder. "Who knew that I'd have a thing for a sexy vegetable and chicken farmer who's also got mad carpentry skills?"

Jordan chuckled. "We've got a lot of work to do to help Ellie get the BnB ready. You'll see those *mad* carpentry skills in action soon."

"Mmm," I moaned and wrapped my arms around his neck, letting my fingers play through the hair at his nape. "The idea of watching you work—surrounded by all the gorgeous grains of wood, the scent of saw dust and varnish in the air, your muscles straining as you saw and hammer and whatever else it is you do…"

Jordan snorted. "You make it sound like a scene straight from carpentry porn."

"Ohhh, I like that," I teased and bit my lip. "Can you invite me—the young, inexperienced apprentice—into your workshop? I'll knock, but the sound of the saw will be too loud, so I'll just walk in. You'll be working with the wood—innuendo very much intended—in *just* your work boots—laces open—and I'll drop to my knees and suck you off before you bend me over your work bench and fuck me." The story was ridiculous, but it had me nearly busting through my zipper.

"Fuck, Marc," Jordan grumbled. "That's a terrible storyline—even for porn—but it's got me so hard, I could fuck you against this wall right this second."

I groaned and pressed my mouth to his, whimpering with want as his tongue snaked in to tease and taste. When we broke apart, both breathless, I smiled as he ran a thumb over my lips. "As fun as that sounds, I think we should likely be somewhat professional and go meet our boarder. Let's raincheck the sex against the barn wall for now—but I have absolutely no qualms about doing it later."

Jordan let loose a growl deep in his chest. "We've got three months to do anything and everything you want to do." He kissed me again—I swore right then and there I'd *never* tire of that man's kisses and no one would *ever* own my lips the way he did—and then pulled me from the barn wall. "Come on, let's go meet your boarder. We'll play the polite hosts for a while, and then we can feign exhaustion or paperwork or something and spend the rest of the night upstairs."

We walked from around the barn and saw a man sitting by the pond.

"Hi," I called out. "Are you Mr. Smith?"

He glanced up from his phone in surprise, but smiled. "Yes. My car broke down and Ms. Kingsley allowed me to pay for a room for the night. Are you Marcus?"

"Marc, yes. I'm Ellie's grandson." I shook his hand and motioned to Jordan. "This is her neighbor, Jordan Moore. He's done most of the carpentry around here, so if you see something you like, be sure to take his card. He's open to custom orders."

Jordan blushed, but shook Mr. Smith's hand.

"Can we get you anything?" I asked. Hospitality such as Gran's wasn't something that came naturally to me, but I forced the question because I knew it was what she would have done.

"No, thank you. Ms. Kingsley said there was a box dinner in the fridge for me. I'll warm that up later. I thought I'd sit here for a while longer before going in to eat, watch some television, and take a shower before bed." Mr. Smith gestured toward the pond. "I don't know how people live here full-time, but the peacefulness is definitely nice."

I nodded. "The hall shower near your room is all yours. We don't have any other guests tonight."

"We'll be working on the property for the next little bit," Jordan added. "If you need anything, just come find us. We'll check in if you're in the kitchen or living room when we come inside. If not, we'll see you in the morning."

"I'm hoping to be able to pick my car up early; they had the part so it should be a quick fix. Ms. Kingsley said there's cereal and some biscuits for breakfast. I should be good to go." Mr. Smith smiled politely. "I know the BnB isn't actually open for guests, so I really appreciate the room."

"Glad we could help." I gave a nod and turned to follow Jordan.

We spent the next hour walking the property. Jordan had grabbed a little tool satchel from his truck and made little fixes on a gate, a bench by the little creek, the handrail of the bridge, and made note to replace one of the wooden slats on the bridge before the official opening.

As he worked, I watched in fascination. "How do you know how to fix all this shit?"

Jordan smiled and winked. "I feel like I was born knowing how to fix shit and work with my hands, but in reality, I learned a lot from my parents. They had me working with the chickens and vegetables as soon as I could walk. Dad gave me my first real toolset when I was five—until then, I toddled around after him carrying my little fake wooden tools—and I was *fixing* things right alongside him from that point on."

I shook my head. "I can't even imagine just looking at something, seeing it's broken, *knowing* how to fix it, and actually being *able* to fix it. You could give me a drawing, every piece of material, and the tools needed, and I'd still have no idea what I was doing."

"Nah, I bet you could learn." Jordan glanced to the row of handcrafted bird houses and then turned to look at the various bird feeders around the property. "You should let me teach you how to make a birdhouse or bird feeder."

I snorted. "What exactly would I use it for? My apartment is in a high-rise building. Definitely no birds hanging around and no place to put it."

Jordan shrugged. "You could leave it for Ellie."

I looked over my shoulder to the birdhouses. "I'll make a birdhouse. They're cute."

"Definitely. They're pretty easy." Jordan hefted the satchel on his shoulder. "We need to pick up some of these limbs; a lot fell during an ice storm this winter. Some of the others fell in an early thunderstorm last month."

Jordan grabbed a wheelbarrow from its place against the fence. We started at the back of the property and worked our way toward the house while filling the cart with twigs and limbs.

"My girl at the salon is going to wonder what the hell I've been doing when I finally get back in for a manicure," I commented as my fingernail caught on a limb. I dug a piece of wood from under the nail.

"You get manicures?" Jordan frowned.

"Yeah, at least once a month if not more. And a pedicure." I cocked my head. "Does that make you think less of me? Makes me less manly?"

Jordan's eyes went wide. "Oh, no. Nothing like that." He blushed. "Do you get colored polish?" He ducked his head. "I'll admit, I have zero idea what a manicure and a pedicure even are."

I smiled. "Oh, my sweet country boy." I took his hand in mine. "You'd love it. They soak your hands and feet, push back your cuticles, trim excess skin, cut and file your nails, and give a mini-massage. It feels amazing. Some guys get color. Some get just a clear coat. I don't get anything on my toes, but I'll get a matte coat on my fingers." I rubbed my thumbs against his palm and grinned at his tiny growl.

"That feels amazing." Jordan shook his head. "No way I could go to the nail place here in Kingsley. I'd be laughed out on my ass."

I leaned in and kissed his cheek. "I'll give you a manicure. I'm not a professional, but it will give you an idea of how great it is." With my hand wrapped around his neck, I pressed my forehead against his. "Maybe you can take a trip to Rockhurst and I'll take you to my spa. They're amazing."

Jordan closed his eyes and sighed. "Pretty sure there's no place in the city for a country bumpkin like me."

"Not true. I'd love to show you around." My heart fluttered. Since when did I want to play host to a tourist gawking around the big city? *Since it's Jordan, not just a tourist.* I cleared my throat and tried to push away the tug on my heart. "What do we do with all these sticks?" I asked and Jordan seemed as relieved and disappointed as I was with the change in conversation.

He took a step back and cleared his throat. "We'll toss these on the stack. Ellie likes to have a few campfires through the season." Jordan gestured toward the pile of sticks in the field next to Gran's house.

Once we were done, Jordan tossed his satchel in the truck and grabbed a different bag. "Are you okay with me staying?" he asked quietly. "If not, I get it, since there's a guest."

I wrapped my arms around his neck and kissed him. "I'm totally fine with it."

The low rumble and shrill whistle of a passing train broke the peaceful silence.

"Ugh, I hate that train," I grumbled.

"Nah, if you're here long enough, you get used to it."

"It's just so *loud*." I wrinkled my nose as we walked

toward the house. "And I swear it goes by like twenty times a day."

Jordan chuckled. "Sometimes it's about that many, but usually not until harvest time. More like ten times a day on average."

I huffed. "Ridiculous."

Jordan smiled.

We found Mr. Smith in the kitchen warming up the box dinner Gran had left for him. The three of us made polite conversation as Jordan and I put together our own dinner.

"Is it okay if I take my food to the living room?" Mr. Smith asked.

"Sure. Just please clean up any spills."

A while later, once Jordan and I had enjoyed leftover noodles and mashed potatoes, we cleaned up the kitchen.

We wandered into the living room.

"You good?" I asked Mr. Smith. "Need anything?"

He glanced between Jordan and me. "I'm good. Going to shower and head to my room soon."

I gave a nod. "Well, we'll be in the upstairs quarters."

Jordan and I turned to head toward the stairs.

"Um," Mr. Smith called out.

We turned.

"Are you two together?"

My breath caught and I felt Jordan tense as we hesitated.

"It's cool if you are," Mr. Smith offered.

With a sigh of relief, I nodded. "We are."

The boarder nodded. "I thought so."

There was an awkward silence and just as I started to turn to leave again, he spoke again. "I'm not gay; my wife will happily attest to that." He eyed me and Jordan and licked his lips. "But I'm not against a bit of play time if you guys are interested."

Once again, my breath caught in my throat. "Oh, um…"

Jordan cleared his throat. "We're kinda a new thing. And since this is a place of business, we'll have to pass for now."

I nodded. "Yeah, what he said."

Mr. Smith smirked and nodded. "Fair enough. You have a good evening, gentlemen."

Jordan and I turned and headed up the stairs.

We reached my room and I ushered Jordan in without a word, closing the door behind us. I turned to Jordan with wide eyes and my mouth gaped. "Oh my God, did the boarder just offer us a threesome?"

Jordan chuckled and rubbed a hand against the back of his neck. "It would appear so."

"Wow. Gotta say, I did *not* see that one coming. There are about a million things I would have guessed would have happened before that." I snorted and rolled my eyes. "Holy shit. I've been propositioned before, but never one that shocked me so much." It wasn't even the fact that the guy offered a threesome; it was more that he was a paying customer in my Gran's house when he did it.

And I wasn't even the least bit interested? That wasn't like me.

Jordan cocked his head. "I'd totally understand if you wanted to take him up on his offer."

My eyes bugged out of my head. "You want to have a threesome with him?" My cock stirred a bit, but my heart squirmed sourly. Was that jealousy?

Holy shit. What was wrong with me?

"No, I don't think that's my speed." Jordan ducked his head. "But I'd get it if you want to hook up with him. He was attractive and you're kinda in a forced dry spell, so I'm okay with it if that's what you'd want."

I frowned. "Do *you* want to hook up with him? If I wasn't here, would you *play* with him?"

Jordan shook his head. "No, not here. And getting

involved with a straight, married guy—or supposedly straight —doesn't seem like a good idea."

"Do you *want* me to go to him? Leave you here in my bed while I go fuck another man?" The words scratched their way from my throat and my stomach churned.

SIX

JORDAN

"No, I don't. But I'm not going to stop you from something you want. I have no ownership, no right to ask you to be with only me." The words burned and my nails dug into my palms; I wanted to go find Mr. Smith and scratch his damn eyes out for having the nerve to even look at Marc. But I had no right.

Marc smiled and stepped close to me. "I guess it's time we had that chat about what this is going to be like for the next three months. But my first thing is that I want it monogamous between us. It may be a short time, but I'm not up for sharing." He wrapped his arms around my neck. "I've had several quick-fuck hook-ups—always safe, protected, consensual—and I've had a few brief flings. But I've always known that, if I was to be in a relationship, I'd need it to be committed." He grimaced. "I'm sorry, I know it's a temporary arrangement, but I can't be sharing you with other men."

My heart soared and I breathed a sigh of relief. "I'm completely okay with that. I've never been in a relationship, but I'm not the type to share." I frowned. "I guess, if I was in a long-term, loving relationship, *maybe* I could give that to my partner if that was something they really wanted. But I have no interest in sharing you." I snaked an arm around Marc's waist. "It may be selfish, but if I only get you for three months, I want every moment we have together to be just us."

"Then we're on the same page." Marc leaned in and brushed his lips over mine. "Plus, even *I* steer clear of the *I'm not gay, but I'm down to play* type of guy and married men. Both are a recipe for disaster, but together? Definitely a hard no."

I pulled Marc in closer and kissed him deeply. The heat between us was instant and I captured his moan with my lips. "Showers? Then chat? Then whatever we decide?"

Marc nodded. "You take the shower in here. I'll go to the hall bathroom." He bit his lip. "Um, would it be presumptuous if I took time to prep?"

I pressed my hips against him and groaned. "I think it would be a very smart decision. See you in thirty minutes?"

We separated and Marc headed to the hallway bathroom with a duffel bag and nothing but a pair of underwear. When he was out of the room, I took my head in my hands and breathed deeply.

Holy shit.

Was I really doing this?

Hook-ups were easy. I almost never saw the guy again. And I most definitely didn't care about him before or after. The sex was always hard and quick. No strings. No connections. Not much foreplay aside from some oral, then I fucked him while he stroked himself. We both enjoyed it. End of story.

But this?

This was with a man I'd spend almost every day with for the next three months. A man I'd already grown to care for. A man I wanted more than a quick hook-up with. There were so many things I'd never experienced with a man and I'd had no problems with those things. *Before.* Before Marc. Now, I wanted it all. With him. Hand jobs, blow jobs, rimming, toys, hard and fast, soft and slow, and everything in between.

I blew out a breath I hadn't realized I'd been holding and stared at the bed.

Would Marc want these three months to be like a string of hook-ups? No connections? Just sex? I swallowed thickly. I'd have a very hard time with that.

But would boyfriends with a time limit be any better?

My heart flipped me off as if to say *I told you this was a bad idea. I'm going to be in shreds. But did you listen? Of course not. You let your dick lead the way. So, now you and your dick are on your own. Figure it out.*

I rolled my eyes. I knew what my heart was saying and I completely understood.

But my cock was at least half-hard already—which seemed to be a natural state any time Marc was nearby, even if sex wasn't the topic of conversation—and I longed to have him in my arms and in the bed as soon as possible.

We'd have to communicate what we were comfortable with and play it by ear with how far and how deep our sexual relationship traveled.

I shook my head and hurried to the bathroom.

I jumped into the shower and washed all over before paying close attention to my cock, balls, and ass. I froze. Marc was prepping which meant he assumed he'd be bottoming. A good assumption, but would he also want me to prep? I didn't have any supplies for that. Did I want to bottom? My cock twitched in my hand. Guess I had my answer.

I'd always topped because it was what the men I hooked up with expected. And I was fine with that. But the idea of bottoming for Marc had me hard and wanting.

Another point that we'd need to talk about.

But for the time being, I'd top. And figure out what all went into prepping. I huffed at myself. *Duh*. I knew what prepping entailed. I'd just never *done* it. But I wanted to—for Marc.

I needed to get out of my head. My anxiety was skyrocketing with all of my thoughts. I stroked my cock a few times, did one more soap and rinse of the vital parts, and stood under the steaming water until my heartrate slowed to a little less than thumping.

Marc—in only a pair of boxer briefs—was rummaging through a basket on the bed when I walked out of the bathroom. He looked up at me—his eyes scanning me from head to toe—and smiled proudly. "Gran doesn't have a matte clear coat, but I can at least work with your cuticles and massage your hands." He patted the bed.

Feeling awkward as hell—but also hornier than I'd ever been—I climbed onto the bed.

"Lean against the pillows and spread your legs," Marc said.

"For a manicure?" But I moved to where he directed.

"I need to hold your hands in front of me as if they were my own. If I'm facing you, I get all turned around and can't do it right. I'd be a terrible nail tech." He gathered his materials and shifted to sit between my legs. After dropping the tools on the bed, he pulled my arms around his torso and picked up my right hand. "Okay, since you're fresh from the shower, you don't need to soak. I'm just going to push back your cuticles and trim any excess skin."

With Marc's warm back pressed against my chest, his trim body wedged between my legs, and his gentle hands working with my fingers, I had no option but to sigh and lean back against the headboard.

"So," Marc began, "we decided we're going to be

monogamous during this whole thing. What else do we want to talk about?"

"Is it secret? Do we tell Ellie?" I asked.

"What's your take on that?"

I shrugged. "I guess I lean a bit more toward keeping it secret. Ellie is my best friend. It's kinda weird to have her know I'm fucking her grandson."

Marc snorted. "Agreed. Awkward to be like, 'Hey, Gran, thanks for introducing me to Jordan. Gonna spend the next three months letting him dick me over *real* good.'"

I laughed. "True. Okay, so we don't tell her."

Marc paused for just a moment. "But we don't flat out lie. If she asks, we tell her."

"I'm good with that. She'd be pissed if we lied. And I'm the one who will be left here with her wrath." My stomach clenched.

"What else?" Marc asked as he continued to press back my cuticles. "Top? Bottom? Vers?"

My tongue was suddenly thick. "Um, I usually top."

Marc turned his head to catch my eyes. "But?" he asked with a grin.

With my face on fire, and my dick begging for friction, I cleared my throat. "I'm interested in bottoming. If that's something you'd be good with. I've only ever topped—mostly because all the guys I hook up with just automatically expect it. Honestly, I don't know that I'd trust many of them to take me. Those interactions are always fast and hard, not a lot of time for a first-time bottom."

Marc took a deep breath.

"But I can totally be an exclusive top if that's better for you. It's what I'm used to." My chest tightened; I shouldn't have even brought it up.

"No, I'm good with topping. I'm completely vers. If I'm being honest, I may lean a bit more toward bottoming, but

I'm very interested in topping you." He switched to my left hand. "Just nervous. I've never topped a virgin."

I snorted. "I've had fingers in my ass, I promise I won't break. You won't ruin me."

Marc's head dropped back against my shoulder with a moan. "What else have you had in your ass?" he whispered gruffly as the manicured paused.

"Oh, um, you mean like toys?"

Marc nodded.

"No, never used them. Like I said, the guys I hook-up with are hard and quick. I usually don't even stay at the room we rent. No time for toys or cuddling." My heart hurt with how badly I wanted those things. Since when had I let myself want more? And now that I'd let myself admit to wanting more—and found it with Marc—I only got to have it for the blink of an eye.

"Would you be interested?" Marc's words were breathy and I knew he could feel my heart beating against his back.

"In toys? Yeah, I think so. I don't know that I want to get *super* kinky. But I'm not against using some to play around."

"What about cuddling?" Marc asked.

I swallowed thickly. "I'm used to sex without it."

"But do you *want* sex with no cuddling?" he pressed.

"With them? I have no interest in cuddling." I answered gruffly.

"And with me?" Marc applied lotion to my right hand and began to rub.

I closed my eyes. This was why it was going to hurt so badly when he left. "With you? I want you in my day-to-day, in my bed, in my arms, and I don't want to let go until you have to leave."

As if pleased *and* troubled by that answer, Marc shifted and stayed quiet for a moment before he moved on. "What are some things you *want* to try? What about hardline no's?"

"I've never done rimming. Given or received. So, I think I'd like to try that if you're okay with it."

Marc's sharp intake of breath went straight to my cock. "You've *never* rimmed? Why?" He continued to work the muscles in my hand.

I shrugged. "I guess it's a lot more intimate than a quick hook-up allows for. And I'm always safe with those guys. Rimming without protection is something I can only see me doing when I have the time and with someone I trust."

"We both know we're clear, so I think we definitely need to introduce you to the joys of rimming. You want to give or receive?" He switched to my left hand and I groaned as he worked his thumb into the fleshy part of my palm.

"Both?" I choked out.

"Totally doable." Marc applied more pressure as he continued to rub in the lotion. "What about positions and locations?"

I groaned. A conversation that basically boiled down to mechanics shouldn't have been sexy, but having his body pressed against mine while talking about toys and rimming and positions was definitely getting me hot. "In the shower? Against a wall? Outside?" I shrugged. "The guys I fuck are usually on their hands and knees or riding me. I'm good with those."

"Open to others?" Marc asked.

"Sure. Never done it face-to-face; seems a bit too intimate with someone I don't even know." My mind imagined Marc on his back, legs spread, me leaning in to kiss him, as my hips surged and thrust my cock deep in his ass.

Marc chuckled. "From the feel of that monster pressing against my back, maybe you'd like to try it that way?"

"Maybe. But only if we both want it that way." I clenched my jaw; I wanted to roll Marc to his back and take him right then.

"I like the idea of sex with you outside. Not around the chickens, though. I don't want them to get the wrong idea about me."

We both laughed.

"What else? What haven't we covered?" Marc asked.

"Is this a three-month string of hook-up type sex? I realize we aren't *boyfriends* or anything, but are we just doing wham-bam-thank-you type sex?" The words spilled in a rush. "I'm good with either way, just need to know."

"If you want it to be a string of hook-ups, that's okay with me," Marc answered as he tossed his tools in the basket and moved it to the floor before rolling to face me. "But," he whispered against my ear, "I've never really had the experience of sex with the same guy over and over. I think I'd like to approach it as more than just hook-ups." His lips teased along my jawline. "I get that we need to keep emotions out of it. I'm not looking to fall in love and settle down. But that doesn't mean that every sexual encounter has to be like sex with a stranger."

"So, we just have fun and do what feels right?" The words clawed their way past a lump in my throat. *He* wasn't looking to fall in love and settle down, but that was what my heart longed for. And damn if I wasn't already feeling halfway there. With a man who just wanted fun sex for a few months before he left.

"Sounds perfect to me." Marc feathered his lips over mine. "I'd really love to get your cock between my lips again."

I groaned and dropped my head back as my hips thrust up. "Go for it. But don't make me come."

"Oh, hell no. You're not coming until you're buried in my ass."

My eyes flew open. "Shit. I didn't bring condoms or lube.

I have some at home, but didn't even think about it. I can go get them."

Marc laughed. "Got it covered." He sealed his lips over mine and dipped his tongue in to tease and taste. Then, with kisses and swirls of his tongue, he made his way down my neck, my chest, my stomach, until he reached the waistband of my boxers. Fiery eyes met mine in question and I nodded.

He smiled and licked his lips as he uncovered my already leaking cock.

"Mmm," Marc moaned. "Been thinking about sucking you ever since the river." His tongue teased my head before dipping into my slit.

My hips surged upward when Marc's hot mouth engulfed my length. He sucked and tongued as my hips thrust my cock gently in and out. When my balls began to tingle, I pushed him away.

"Could totally come like that," I warned. "But I've got more I want to do."

Marc licked his lips. "Sometime soon, I want you to fuck my face and make me gag on your dick."

I groaned. "Fuck," I gritted out. "Don't say things like that when I'm trying to pace myself."

Marc laughed.

I peeled his underwear down and immediately took his hard cock in my mouth. I'd been dreaming of his silky skin, his plump head, his salty, bitter flavor.

Marc whimpered and moaned as I sucked him deep, but I wanted more.

"Turn over," I demanded.

He rolled to his stomach and I lifted his hips. Marc spread his legs and I groaned as he presented his hole to me.

With a gentle finger, I caressed the puckered skin and smiled when his breath caught. Slicking my thumb in my mouth, I returned to his hole and softly massaged his entrance as Marc pressed his hips against my touch.

I shifted from my knees to my stomach and took hold of the tops of Marc's thighs, spreading him open even more, and nuzzling my nose against his skin. My lips and tongue teased where his legs met his ass. I tongued the sensitive skin of his taint. And then I allowed myself to taste him in a way I'd never tasted another man.

Marc's moans and whimpers spurred me on as I licked and speared my tongue into his body, the soft skin and tight muscle yielding under my touch.

I reached between Marc's legs and took his rock-hard cock in my fist. As I began to stroke him while tonguing his ass, Marc cried out.

"Too much, gonna come," he warned. "Want you in me." He moved across the bed and yanked open the bedside table drawer. "Threw these in here while you were in the shower. Hope Gran doesn't check my drawers." Then he grimaced. "Oh God, mentioning your grandmother to the man who just had his tongue in your ass is likely very poor form. My bad."

I snorted and grabbed the condom and lube from him. I rolled the latex down my throbbing cock and slicked it with lube. "Let's try that wall sex," I suggested.

Marc bit his lip and groaned. "Lay down with your legs over the side of the bed. I'll straddle you and then you can stand and fuck me against the wall."

I sat on the bed and lay down on my back.

Marc straddled my waist and reached behind to guide my cock to his ass.

My senses went into overload mode as Marc's tight, hot hole opened for me, his grunts and moans filled the air, his face—eyes locked on mine—painted with ecstasy as he lowered himself onto me inch-by-inch, and the scent of our sex permeated the room.

"Fuck," Marc panted, "you feel huge. So good."

I sat up and wrapped my arms around Marc's body as I leaned in to kiss him. I'd never kissed a man *during* sex that I could recall. Before? Yes. Maybe after? But during? That had never happened. Or it wasn't worth remembering.

But kissing Marc, absorbing the magic of his lips and tongue as my throbbing cock was buried in his tight heat, was something I'd remember for the rest of my life. When he was gone, and I was alone, I'd dream of the heady feeling of his arms around my neck, his leaking dick between our bodies, and his ass clenching around my shaft. "Wrap your legs around me," I demanded.

Between kisses and whimpery grunts as my cock thrust into his body, Marc managed to shift enough to wrap his legs around me.

I stood and took three steps to the outside wall. "You good? Can you hold on?"

Marc nodded. "For a while. May have to go back to the bed in a bit."

Relief coursed through me. Fucking him against the wall was hot, but my arms and legs had not been prepared for the extra physical exertion. Using the wall as leverage, I thrust hard and fast as Marc made the most delicious noises and took me deep.

"Fuck, so big, so good," he chanted.

Deciding I liked the angle the bed gave better than the wall, I took us back to the bed. "Ride me? On your knees?" I didn't care what the position, but I needed to fuck him hard and watch him come.

"Let me lean on the bed," Marc suggested as I placed him on the bed.

With a gruff groan, I slid from his body.

He rolled to his stomach and reached behind to spread his ass open. "Fuck me, Jordan."

His lube-slicked and stretched hole was all the invitation I needed as I pressed the swollen head of my cock back into his heat with a groan.

I leaned forward, spreading my body over his as I fucked into his ass.

Over and over I slid in and out, our skin slapping together as his body clung to mine. A tingle traveled from my spine to my balls and I snaked my arms under his chest to hold him tight. "Gonna unload in your ass and then suck you off until you come down my throat."

Marc moaned. "Do it. Come in my ass. Wanna feel your cock explode."

With a few more thrusts, I lost myself as an orgasm roared through me and I shot my hot load in Marc's ass.

Anxious to watch him come, I pulled my still-throbbing dick from his heat and dropped to my knees to take his hard, swollen length deep to the back of my throat. Fondling his balls and teasing his hole, I sucked Marc's cock as he thrust his hips. When I slid a finger deep inside his body, he bucked and shot his salty release onto my waiting tongue with a loud groan.

After licking him clean, I removed the condom from my satisfied dick, wrapped it in a tissue, and tossed it in the trashcan before climbing onto the bed and taking a very soft and cuddly Marc in my arms. "You are loud during sex," I teased. "Or at least when you come."

Marc froze. "Oh God, do you think Mr. Smith heard me? That can't be professional, right?"

I laughed. "No worries, the train was going by just as you came. I doubt he heard you over the whistle."

"Well, that fucking train is at least good for something."

"Wanna shower or sleep?" I asked as I kissed his neck, my arms wrapped around him and my hands caressing his chest.

"Sleep. Then I want you to fuck me again. And maybe

again. We can shower in the morning." Marc's words were thick and heavy as he drifted toward sleep.

"Two more times? Damn, man. Don't forget I'm older than you," I joked.

"I have faith in your abilities. My ass needs more of your cock."

We fell to sleep in our own little warm cocoon.

I WOKE FEELING GLORIOUSLY sore and worn out, but the warm body plastered to my side made me smile.

The first time we'd woken during the night, Marc had pushed me to my back, unrolled a condom down my length, straddled me, and ridden my cock with slow, rocking hips until I thrust up hard as I came. With my cock still throbbing and buried in his ass, Marc had stroked himself and painted his release across my stomach and chest.

With about two hours before sunrise, I'd come to consciousness as Marc's very naked ass rubbed and rocked against my hard shaft.

"You need something, Oxford?" I'd growled in Marc's ear as I thrust my hips, pressing my cock between his cheeks.

"Take me. Just like this," Marc had begged.

I'd reached behind me, blindly groping for the condoms, and made quick work of suiting up. Teasing his tight pucker, I'd groaned at how easily my finger slipped inside. "Still slick," I'd said and spread the leftover lube before spitting on my finger to add a bit more wetness.

Marc had moaned and lifted his top leg, bending it to rest against the bed.

The movement had given me better access to his entrance, and I'd nudged my head against him. Pressing slowly, I'd growled as his body opened for me and grunted when my balls met his skin.

"Go slow," he'd whispered.

"Are you sore?" I'd paused in concern.

"Not bad, just need to take it easy." He'd rocked his hips and whimpered as my cock slid in and out of his body.

Shifting so that his side was pressed against the mattress and my body mostly covered his, I'd lifted and bent my top leg to mirror his position and began to thrust long and slow into him. I'd wrapped my arms around him and captured his ear between my teeth. "Wanna come in you, feel your ass milk my cock," I'd whispered gruffly.

We'd rocked and thrust, groaned and whimpered for several minutes before I'd taken Marc's dick in my fist and started to stroke.

He'd thrown his head back, exposing his neck and crying out as my fist stroked and my cock plunged deep.

With a gentle, teasing bite to the sensitive skin of his neck, I'd given a final thrust and spilled my release with a muffled moan against his shoulder.

Marc had tensed in my arms and grunted as his cock pulsed and coated my fingers.

After a quick clean-up, we'd fallen back to sleep until sunrise.

And that was how I woke up. Warm and happy against Marc's side as Hank announced the dawn of a new day.

"Mmm," Marc grumbled. "Too early. Hank needs to shut the fuck up," he muttered against my chest.

"I'm going to shower and fix breakfast. You can sleep until you smell coffee." I nuzzled my nose against his cheek and pressed a kiss to his lips. "You were fucking amazing last night; you deserve to sleep in."

"Sleep as payment for fabulous sex? I'm down with that." Marc ran a hand up and down my chest before venturing lower and stroking my cock. "Tonight? Your place? Gonna spend all day thinking about swallowing your load."

My dick twitched and I moaned. "If I thought I could survive a fourth round, I'd give it a go, but you wore me out," I teased.

"Don't work too hard today," Marc warned. "I need you ready to go tonight." He pressed a kiss against my lips. "Or maybe I just need you spread out before me so I can slide my dick in your ass and make you come."

That time, my dick gave a valiant effort to stand up and I growled. "The idea of your cock buried in my ass will keep me hard and horny all damn day."

"Perfect. Now go get ready. I need coffee." Marc burrowed into the pillow and mumbled something about rising before the damn sun.

I spent the next twenty minutes showering and getting dressed before slapping Marc's ass on my way out of his room. "Twenty minutes, Oxford."

He grumbled and I'm pretty sure attempted to flip me the bird with his sleepy fingers.

SEVEN

MARC

I COULDN'T HELP the satisfied grin that filled my face as I brushed my teeth, showered, shaved, and pulled on my new work jeans and t-shirt. Donning a flannel button-up, I took a deep breath of the coffee-and-bacon-scented-air and smiled even wider. My ass was deliciously sore, my lips tingled with a slight beard burn from all the kisses, and my dick—while looking forward to later that night—was deeply sated.

I all but bounced down the stairs, ignoring the unfamiliar flutter I felt in my chest when I saw Jordan—ass snug in a pair of jeans, flannel sleeves rolled up—in front of the stove cooking what looked like some sort of eggs and bacon.

He turned toward me with a sparkle in his eyes and a big smile that made my heart do weird things. "Good morning. Look at you dressing all countrified. Keep this up and I won't be able to call you Oxford anymore."

I wrapped my arms around his waist and kissed the side of his neck. "You can call me anything you want." For a brief moment, I thought about how great it would be to find Jordan cooking breakfast in the kitchen every morning. How amazing it would be to look toward a future with him in my bed, by my side. But I pushed the thought away. We'd agreed to three months. Three months only. My life was with the business in Rockhurst. Jordan's life was with his farm in Kingsley. This was a very temporary situation and I needed to keep that in mind. At all times.

"Oxford, sexy, hot-as-hell, absolutely amazing in bed," Jordan whispered as he held me, "just a few of the words I can think of to call you."

"I'm offended. Those make me seem shallow and only worthy of sex," I teased.

Jordan smiled and smacked a kiss against my lips. "How about intelligent, kind, quick learner, and funny thrown in as well?"

I pretended to consider. "I'll accept those words. As long as you remember I'm more than just a pretty face," I joked.

Jordan's face sobered and he pressed his forehead to mine. "I'll never forget that; you're so much more than just a pretty face or amazing in bed. So much more," he whispered.

I swallowed thickly, the seriousness of the moment wrapping me in an unfamiliar—but not unwanted—warmth tinged with fingers of heartbreak and regret. "More than a pretty face, yes. But I think we need to continue working on the amazing-in-bed part. Practice makes perfect." I pushed away the myriad of feelings and pressed a kiss against his lips just as a throat cleared from the doorway.

"Morning, gentlemen," Mr. Smith said.

"Morning," Jordan said as he turned back toward the stove.

A weird thrill went through me when he didn't jump away from me or seem freaked out that the boarder had seen us kissing or hugging.

"Called the shop. My car is ready. They're sending someone to pick me up, so I'll be out of your hair soon." Mr. Smith smiled and placed an overnight bag by the door.

"I'll get you a travel cup of coffee and a couple breakfast sandwiches for the road," Jordan offered.

The three of us made small talk—Mr. Smith acted as if he'd never once made the threesome offer—for the next few minutes as Jordan poured coffee and wrapped up two bacon, sausage, egg, and cheese biscuits.

Mr. Smith waved and promised to suggest Gran's BnB to all of his friends as he headed out the door.

When we were alone, Jordan piled two plates with bacon, omelets, sausage, biscuits, and gravy. "Dig in. We've got a lot of work to do today," he said.

"Are you trying to give me a heart attack?" I asked as I eyed all the food. "This is like carb and fat overload."

"Nah, breakfast is the most important part of the day. We need to fill up for energy all day."

"This is going to make me want a nap." But I slathered butter and strawberry jelly on a biscuit.

I glanced at all of the food and decided to start with the omelet as it was likely the healthiest option since it was protein and filled with veggies. After one bite, I determined that Jordan was not only magical with his lips and cock, but he had a magic touch with omelets as well.

"Oh my God," I moaned, "I've never tasted an omelet this good." I shoveled another bite in my mouth. "What's your secret?"

Jordan smiled as he watched me take two more bites. "You seriously want to know?"

I nodded. "I mean, I don't cook for myself often, but I've got to know your trick."

He cleared his throat as I took the last bite of my omelet. "Fresh eggs."

I froze.

I wanted to get angry and protest, but the rich, savory flavors that danced on my tongue could not be argued. "No shit? The only thing you used that would be different is fresh eggs?"

Jordan smirked and shrugged. "I mean, the veggies are fresh from the garden and I used a bit of lard along with the cooking spray. But the fresh eggs are likely the biggest difference."

I swallowed the last bite and washed it down with a swig of coffee. "I'm man enough to admit when I'm wrong. I will never again argue over fresh eggs. The thought of them not being refrigerated still freaks me out, but they are hands down better than the cold, store-bought ones I've cooked with and tasted."

Jordan raised a brow. "Maybe you can find a farmers market in Rockhurst and get fresh eggs. You can keep them cold; they'll still be better than the store-bought ones."

The reminder of going back to Rockhurst was like a bucket of cold water, but I nodded my head. "Yeah, there are definitely some markets near me on the weekends." I picked up a biscuit and took a bite.

Then I groaned.

"Oh my God."

Jordan laughed. "What now?"

"This jelly tastes just like a strawberry. Like it's just been jellified and spread on my biscuit." I licked a red smear from my finger.

"First, it's not jelly. It's jam."

"What's the difference?" I took another delicious bite.

"Jelly is clearer and stiffer. Jam has more of the fruit in it and is more spreadable. Ellie makes the best homemade strawberry jam."

"With strawberries from your garden?" I asked.

"That batch came from my garden. She'll probably have to get the berries elsewhere this year, I didn't get any strawberries planted." Jordan dunked a biscuit in the creamy sausage gravy.

I cocked my head and frowned. "I don't think I've ever seen a strawberry plant. I mean, I know they grow on some sort of plant. But I've only ever seen them at the store or a market in those basket type containers."

Jordan's eyes went wide. "Okay, that's it. We're planting strawberries. You *can't* go back to Rockhurst without at least seeing a strawberry plant." He wrinkled his nose. "You'll miss the fruit being ripe enough to *pick*, but if we plant soon, you'll at least be able to see the plant bear fruit."

If I wasn't looking so forward to returning to my normal life in the city, I probably would have been bent out of shape at how many times Jordan brought up the fact that I was leaving.

Instead, I just took another bite of the biscuit and savored the explosion of strawberry on my tongue. "I'm going to ask Gran if I can have a jar of this jam to take home."

Jordan laughed. "I'm sure she'd love that. She always makes enough to sell through the season and still have plenty through the winter. I'm sure she'd be thrilled to send you home with some."

Why did my chest burn at the thought of leaving? And why did Jordan seem just fine with me going home?

A MONTH into my time in Kingsley found me completely settled into my new routine. I was up at dawn with Hank's ridiculous noise—I hadn't yet actually stopped bitching about it, but I was at least able to rise earlier than ever before. I looked forward to fresh-egg-omelets. I was learning to be friendly and interact with the guests. I adored spending time with Gran almost daily. And I hadn't had a headache since my arrival.

I was even getting used to that damn train.

Jordan and I spent every day together. We'd planted strawberries—and I hadn't admitted it yet, but I was sad to think I'd never get to see the fruit come on and ripen—and we'd fallen into a perfect rhythm of chores with the chickens, the veggies, and the BnB, while still having time to work on Jordan's carpentry business.

The hothouse veggies were still going strong and the outside garden plants were thriving. I found myself excited every day to see what new things were growing in the gardens.

I'd learned the personalities of most of the chickens. Some were very standoffish, but there were quite a few who loved to socialize. I spent way too much time chatting with the ladies each day. A month ago, the idea of talking to chickens would have made me laugh—no way I would have ever done that—but *now*? I could admit they were good listeners.

The website I'd set up for Jordan had gone live and he'd landed three sales within the first day—my guess was because people at Gran's saw the fine craftsmanship and took his card so they could order as soon as they left—so we were planning a celebration.

Just the two of us.

After dinner with Gran, of course.

The three of us had taken to eating our evening meals together. Sometimes with the guests, sometimes on our own.

When Jordan had told Gran I'd never had bread and gravy or sugar cream pie, she was shocked, dismayed, and determined to fix that issue.

"Ellie wants us to bring several ears of corn so she can fix them with dinner," Jordan commented as he began filling a basket with corn as we finished up our late chores. "How many pieces do you want?"

I wrinkled my nose. "One?"

Jordan frowned. "You don't like fresh sweet corn?"

I shrugged. "I mean, I've had it a couple times. Always seemed kinda chewy and tasteless to me."

Jordan's eyes sparkled. "You definitely haven't had fresh sweet corn. I guarantee you'll be singing a different tune after dinner tonight."

"Fine, I'll take two ears." I rolled my eyes. "It's not a crime to not like corn on the cob."

"I'm putting in more than two pieces each. No one says you *have* to love it, but I'm guessing the corn on the cob you've had is nothing compared to fresh sweet corn."

I gave him a kiss. "Don't get your hopes up. Maybe I just don't like corn."

"Mmhm," Jordan hummed.

"So, after dinner with Gran, what are we doing to celebrate?" I asked.

"We're going to watch a movie outside and sleep out under the stars," Jordan said.

I snorted.

Then I realized he was serious.

"Oh, um. I'm not really the type of person who sleeps outside." I wrinkled my nose.

Jordan smiled. "Don't worry, Oxford. I'll take care of you. But I think it's important you experience all sorts of country-boy activities before you leave. And an outdoor movie and sleeping under the stars is definitely one of those things."

"Can I argue?" I wrapped my arms around his neck and nuzzled his jaw.

"Nope. After all, it's my carpentry business we're celebrating. So, I get to decide."

I scowled. "But *I* made the website. It could be argued that the sales are because of me."

Jordan chuckled. "I thought you said that my work sold itself and the website wouldn't work if my craftsmanship wasn't so fine and amazing?"

I huffed. "Fine. Will there at least be sex involved with this outside movie and sleeping?"

Jordan cocked a brow. "We've been fucking each other's brains out for a month. Do you think I'd miss out on outdoor sex with you?"

I bit my lip and smiled as I thought of the amazing sex we'd been having. Jordan seemed to have taken it as a personal challenge to fuck me in my bed at the BnB and make me come at the same time as the train whistled as often as possible. I didn't *think* Gran knew we were hooking up. But I was possibly wrong.

We spent a lot of nights at Jordan's house. It was easier to be there because we didn't have to keep our hands off each other. Didn't have to time my orgasms with the train whistle. Didn't have to pretend there were reasons for me to be in Jordan's room.

"Okay, as long as I get your cock, I'll put up with sleeping outdoors." I cocked my head. "What are some of the other things you think I need to experience before I leave?" The stupid burn in my chest that always happened when I thought of going back to Rockhurst flamed to life.

"We're going to build that birdhouse. I think we also need to go to a field party, mushroom hunting, and fishing." Jordan laughed at the look on my face. "And you've not experienced country living until you've gotten stuck behind a tractor on your way into town."

"Those things sound…" I wrinkled my nose, "terrible?"

He smirked. "You've got to experience the bad with the

good so when you leave you won't wonder if you're leaving things undone."

I frowned. "Doesn't matter what *things* I experience here; *you're* the only thing I'll miss."

A flash of what looked to be pain crossed Jordan's face, but he smiled to hide it. "You won't miss the omelets? Gran's cooking? Hank's alarm clock at dawn?"

"Nope—at least not Hank. But you've spoiled me with daily sex and *that* will definitely be missed."

"So, the sex is all you'll miss?" Jordan teased.

I swallowed thickly. "We've got two months left. Let's not worry about all of that right now."

Jordan pulled me into a tight hug. "Never hoped for two months to go slow before. But now? I'm praying for time to crawl."

I EYED my yet-to-be-filled plate surrounded by a loaf of homemade white bread, a platter of fried ham, a bowl of white, creamy gravy, and a plate of corn on the cob.

"So, this meal consists of salted meat, chunks of carbohydrates soaked in liquified fat, and chewy, tasteless rows of carbs disguised as a vegetable?" I wrinkled my nose.

"I never knew you were so unexposed to country cooking." Gran clicked her tongue. "I also never knew you were such a snob."

Jordan snorted.

"It may not be the healthiest meal, but it's one you've never had and you should definitely try it. Don't you have some sort of food in the city that you think everyone should at least try once?" Gran cocked her brow.

"Sushi," I answered without hesitation.

"Okay, consider my homemade bread and ham gravy the

country sushi." Gran pushed the loaf of bread my way. "Now, I'll tell you that most don't use homemade bread and that's okay. But I have bread ready at all times, so it makes sense to use it."

"What are the guests eating? Can I opt to eat with them?" I glanced toward the formal dining room.

"They are eating the same. We're eating in here tonight because I had a feeling you'd throw a fit." Gran pointed at the bread. "Let's go. Food's getting cold."

Jordan took two slices of bread and began tearing them into chunks.

"Do I have to eat the crust?" I whined as I took two slices.

"You are such a child," Jordan teased.

"If you're adverse to the crust, you can take it off." Gran rolled her eyes and began to fix her own plate.

I removed the crust and tore the soft bread into pieces as Jordan had done.

After Jordan had spooned the creamy white gravy over the bread on his plate, he handed the bowl to me with a smirk. And a twinkle in his eye that had my stomach and heart doing all kinds of flips and flops.

I frowned, but spooned gravy over the bread on my plate. This meal seemed so wrong; there was no way I was going to like it. Maybe I could sneak a biscuit and strawberry jam later.

"Get some butter and salt on your corn before it's cold," Gran directed.

I took one ear of corn.

"Take two. It's easier to get them both ready."

"He doesn't think he likes corn," Jordan piped up.

Gran's eyes went wide. "What? Fresh sweet corn is one of God's gifts to your mouth."

I snorted and bit back a comment about Jordan's cock being the real gift to my mouth, but Jordan kicked me under the table. I shrugged. "I've tried it a couple times. It's just always been tasteless and chewy."

"Not fresh and cooked too long. Boy, you're going to eat your words along with multiple ears of corn. I'd put money on it." Gran shoved the butter my way.

I grabbed a knife and began to smear the butter onto two ears of corn. "You should be happy that I've fallen in love with strawberry jam and real butter. Isn't that enough?" I was throwing out all of the margarine in my apartment when I got home; real butter was hands-down better.

"And fresh eggs?" Jordan teased.

I wrinkled my nose. "I like them and I'll buy them. But I'm not claiming to have fallen in love with them." I sprinkled a bit of salt on my corn. "Okay, which of these travesties should I start with?"

Gran rolled her eyes. "Bread and gravy first. Then a few bites of corn."

I followed her directions.

The salty flavor of the creamy gravy mixed perfectly with the soft, yeasty bread as my mouth filled with an unimaginably delicious flavor.

I groaned.

Jordan and Gran smirked.

I took another bite and savored it before swallowing with a scowl. "How is this so good? It's chunks of bread covered in liquid fat. It should be disgusting."

"And yet, it's not," Gran quipped with a nod. "Try the corn."

Before the bread and gravy, I doubted Jordan and Gran's food suggestions. Now, I wasn't so sure.

Following Jordan's lead, I picked up the ear of corn and took a bite.

Each crisp kernel of corn burst with sweet, buttery, salty

flavor. My tongue delighted in the sweet and salty mixture along with the perfect texture as I chewed.

Again, I groaned.

Gran and Jordan lost it and laughed, not even attempting to hide their rude reactions behind their napkins.

Choosing to ignore them, I dug into my meal and enjoyed every damn bite.

By the time I finished my fifth ear of corn, I moaned and wiped my mouth.

"Glad I picked more than two ears for you?" Jordan teased.

I held up my hand and took a swallow of tea—unsweetened, of course; that particular aversion wasn't changing. Ever. "It appears that being banished to Kingsley was as much for my mental and physical health as it was for my ability to admit when I'm wrong; it seems that's all I've been doing lately. At least where food is related." I took another drink. "Fine. Fresh eggs are better. Homemade strawberry jam is superior to store-bought jelly. Real butter is delicious. Bread and gravy is a fucking plate of happiness. And fresh sweet corn is nectar for the gods, truly ambrosia. Happy?"

Jordan and Gran just smiled.

"As long as you are willing to try new things and admit when you like them, I'm good." Gran patted my hand before she stood.

"Just glad we can give you all the country experiences." Jordan glanced toward the counter where Gran was cutting slices of pie before he reached over and gave my thigh a squeeze.

"Oh my God, Gran," I groaned. "There's no way I can eat pie right now."

"Boy, you ate so much corn, I doubt you'll be ready for pie before morning. I'm taking out a few slices and sending the rest of it with Jordan. Since you boys are celebrating tonight, you can have pie and coffee when you're ready for a snack." She smiled with a quick shrug. "Or for breakfast. Whichever."

For just a moment, I panicked. She knew. Didn't she? Maybe? Maybe not?

"Thanks, Ellie. We'll help with dishes and then go get the movie set up." Jordan stood and didn't listen when Gran argued about us helping. "I was telling Marc that he needs to go fishing, attend a field party, and go mushroom hunting before he leaves."

Gran nodded. "Agreed. Those are perfect." Then she laughed. "I can't wait to hear about how irked he gets when he gets stuck behind a tractor on his way into town."

"Hey," I exclaimed. "*He* is right here. And I'm all relaxed and Zen and shit these days. No tractor is going to irk me."

Jordan and Gran glanced at each other and burst out laughing.

I put a hand to my chest. "I'm offended. Both of you should have more faith in me."

They just kept laughing.

"I CAN'T BELIEVE you have your own outdoor movie screen." I helped hang the sheet on the side of Jordan's work shed.

"A projector and a sheet," Jordan said, "it's not exactly high-tech."

I shrugged with a smile. "I guess I just didn't think about having things like this all the way out here."

"We're not less fortunate or going without, Oxford." Jordan chuckled. "I ordered the projector from Amazon. The sheet, too. We can get pretty much anything delivered or pick it up at a store if we're willing to drive a bit. Delivery might not be next day; we might not have every convenience right around the corner, but it's not like we're suffering."

I paused. "No, it's not...okay, yeah, I guess that's kinda how I was looking at it." I wrinkled my nose. "Sorry."

Jordan caught me around the waist and pulled me in close. "It's okay. It's a common misconception. But we really are doing just fine out here in the sticks."

I nodded. "Yeah, I can see that. It's just hard to adjust from *I'll just go down the block and get sushi* or *I can order today and have it delivered by tonight.* But I'm beginning to realize that the slower and more relaxed ways out here aren't *bad*, just different." I pressed kisses against his stubbly cheek. "There are things I definitely miss from the city, but I can't say that I've missed the tension and stress; it's been amazing to be without headaches. The fresh air, physical labor, and sense of accomplishment after a long day of work are growing on me. I'm even getting kinda used to the slower pace."

"Well, I'm getting used to having you here with me." Jordan smacked a kiss against me and then let me go as if attempting to distance himself from me.

How different would our relationship be if I was staying indefinitely?

I shook my head. That wasn't happening, so it was pointless to even think about.

"So, we watch the movie on the side of the shed, but where do we sit?" I asked. *Please don't say we're sitting on the ground.*

Jordan laughed. "Relax, Oxford. I won't make you dirty your pretty ass on the ground," he joked as if reading my mind—and I kinda liked that he knew me that well.

"You like my pretty ass," I whispered as I snaked an arm around his neck and nuzzled against his ear.

"I love your pretty ass," Jordan growled.

Time stood still.

It was just a word, he didn't mean anything more than he enjoyed fucking me.

Jordan cleared his throat and gripped my ass as he kissed me deeply.

The awkwardness of the moment slipped away as easily as Jordan's tongue slipped between my lips.

Just as I was ready to say fuck the movie, Jordan broke the kiss. "We'll sit in the back of my truck. Can you get the projector and my laptop while I pull the truck around?"

While I gathered the technology, I realized two things. One, I'd found great relief in not being tied to my phone and laptop; I kept up with some emails, but it had been great to unplug a bit. At least temporarily. Two, I hadn't once had any issues with slow internet. One of the biggest problems I thought I'd have with the country location turned out to be no issue at all.

I met Jordan outside and he cocked his head.

"What are you thinking? You look deep in thought."

"Just that I figured internet would be a huge problem out here, but I just realized that I've not once had any issues. How is that?" I scowled.

Jordan chuckled. "Well, I will say that Kingsley is lucky in several ways. One, we are kinda in the middle of a few larger towns and many of our folk take advantage of the bigger towns' internet services."

"And two?"

He smiled. "And Ellie recently took steps to provide the BnB and surrounding areas—mainly my place—with top-notch internet. She knew it would be a perk for guests. It also helps her with staying in touch with Rockhurst." Jordan winked. "Personally, I think she's laying plans for getting your grandfather to move out here permanently. The really good internet is a huge step."

"Well, that at least explains how your internet and Gran's is so great." I thought for a moment. "I think Gramps would love to be out here for good. They could always visit Rockhurst as needed."

Jordan cocked a brow and a look of longing flashed over his face. But he cleared his throat and gestured toward the bed of his truck. "Your movie seating and bedroom for the night awaits."

My eyes went wide. "Oh my God, that's amazing. If this is *roughing* it, I can totally get behind it."

Jordan laughed. "No, Oxford. This is *not* roughing it. But it's likely the roughest I'll get you to agree to for a while. Real roughing it would be sleeping on the ground, lucky if you have a sleeping bag, no bathroom, no kitchen, and cooking over a fire."

I grimaced. "Eeeww, no thanks. *This* is what I will forever expect of roughing it now."

Jordan had stuffed an air mattress into the bed of his truck, covered it with blankets and pillows, placed candles on the toolbox that stretched the width of the truck bed, and provided two bottles of water.

"I'll get a thermos of coffee and the pie. Change into something suitable to sleep in. Meet you here in twenty." Jordan smacked a kiss on my mouth. "Showtime is in thirty."

By the time we met back at the truck, Jordan and I were both in lounge pants and t-shirts. The air was chilly, but I figured the blankets and body heat would take care of that.

"Climb aboard," Jordan invited with a sweep of his hand. "Shoes off first, of course."

I toed off my shoes and hopped onto the lowered tailgate.

Jordan did the same, placed the coffee and pie on the toolbox, and then moved to where the laptop and projector were on the roof of the truck's cabin.

"Okay, here's the big decision." Jordan waggled his brows. "What movie?"

My eyes went wide. "Oh, we're actually watching a movie?"

Jordan chuckled. "Yes, Oxford. We're actually watching a movie, my little horndog."

I laughed. "Who says horndog?" I pursed my lips. "I thought watching a movie was a code for sex."

"Oh, there's going to be sex." Jordan winked. "But a movie first. Watching a movie on the side of a shed while cuddled in a truck bed is something you need to experience."

My heart fluttered and I smiled. "Okay. So, what are our movie options?"

Jordan shrugged. "Pretty much anything you can think of."

I scanned my brain trying to think of a movie we should watch, but then I had an idea. "How about this? I'll pull up a top one hundred list of movies and you pick a number. Whatever number you pick is the movie we watch."

"Perfect." Jordan nodded and seemed to be legit pleased with the way we were spending the evening.

I typed *Top 100 Best Movies of All Time* into the search box on my phone. I clicked on the first list and scrolled through the movies. "Wow, this is quite the variety. Okay, pick a number between one and one hundred."

Jordan cocked his head to the side. "This is a lot of pressure. One bad choice and I could be sentencing us to two hours of rubbish."

"Nah, these are supposedly the one hundred best movies of all time, so they must be good. Come on, come on. I need a number; the suspense is killing me." I nudged him.

Jordan hummed for a second. "Okay, here we go." He took a deep breath. "Going with lucky number seventy-six."

"What makes seventy-six lucky?" I prodded.

"I don't know! What did I pick?"

I scrolled through the list until I reached seventy-six. Then threw my head back in laughter.

"What? What is it? Is it terrible? I can make another choice."

I smiled and showed him the screen of my phone. "I'm totally on board because I actually haven't watched this."

"*Brokeback Mountain*?" Jordan chuckled. "Well then, okay. I've not watched it either. Let me buy it."

"Aww, we're both *Brokeback Mountain* virgins. So sweet."

Jordan purchased the movie, made sure the projector was showing correctly on the screen, and then settled next to me on the mattress. He put an arm around my shoulder, pulled me close, and kissed the top of my head.

I sighed. "I'll never admit it to the city slickers, but this is kinda amazing."

The movie turned out to be good.

Sad. Very sad. But good.

After the credits rolled, Jordan packed the technology away in a case. "You ready for coffee and pie?"

I groaned. "I shouldn't be ready to eat anything else for a week after how much I shoved in my mouth at dinner."

Jordan smirked. "But?"

I huffed. "But pie and coffee sound delicious. Bring it on."

He went to work and soon we were seated, nestled close on the pillows, a tray-like board over our laps with two mugs of steaming coffee and two plates of pie. "Don't wiggle; we'll be wearing the coffee."

"What kind of pie did you call this?" I eyed it suspiciously. Even in the dusky evening, I could tell it wasn't like pie I'd seen before. "I've had apple, chocolate, and coconut pie. That's the extent of my pie experience."

"*This* is sugar cream pie and it's to die for." Jordan forked up a bite and held it to my lips.

Forgoing the argument that wanted to pass my lips, I tentatively took the bite from the fork and let the flavors melt on my tongue. The flaky, faintly salty, crust mixed perfectly with the smooth, creamy, sweet filling. "Oh my God, that's amazing."

"Eat your own," Jordan teased. "That's the only bite of mine you're getting."

"Oh, so you feed me when you think I maybe won't like it. But I'm on my own when I want more?" I took a bite of my own piece and moaned. "Oh my God, so good."

We spent the next couple minutes savoring what had possibly become my favorite dessert and sipping coffee.

"The movie was sad, huh?" I mused a few moments later as we moved our empty mugs and plates to the side and pushed the tray off our laps.

Jordan nodded, his features serious in the moonlight. "Yeah, it was. I really liked the story overall, but it was sad."

"I'm grateful to live in a time and area where I can be myself," I mused.

Jordan sighed. "Yeah, I guess I have it better than they did. But am I really all that much better off? I guess I'm not hiding behind a wife and sneaking around, but I'm not openly gay."

My heart clenched at the emotion in his words. "Gran knows. I know. I'm sure Gramps knows. I get what you're saying, but I also don't know that I'd say you're *hiding*. You just haven't felt the need to tell the whole town. Small towns are rough. I'm out, but I'm in a city with hundreds of thousands of people. I have a cloak of anonymity in many ways. With a town this small, you don't have that." I took his hand. "I get the feeling you're not exactly lying to others or yourself, just not coming out and announcing anything that's really not their business."

Jordan gave my hand a squeeze. "I'm like Jack. He wanted

to settle down and have a nice life with the man he loved. Instead, he ended up miserable and…"

"Hey, you're not a character in a movie. You're a real-life person with friends and family and a job you love. You live in a beautiful area. You're talented beyond belief." I leaned my head on his shoulder. "And I happen to think you're hooking up with one of the hottest, most eligible bachelors in a two-hundred-mile radius."

Jordan chuckled. "Is that so? Is he also humble?"

I shrugged. "He's just honest." I shifted to kiss Jordan's chin. "I'm just saying that Ennis and Jack's story doesn't have to be ours."

Jordan and I tensed as my words filled the cool night air.

Our story.

Shit.

"I mean, neither of us have to end up like them. We're of a different time, we live in a different area. I don't think either of us are going to marry a woman and have children." The words poured from me as I tried to hide the fact that I'd alluded to Jordan and I having a future.

His words were low and gruff. "I convince myself I'm happy. My life is good. It truly is. I don't really *want* for anything. I have everything I need and I can find sexual fulfillment when I want it."

I knew he had more to say.

"But there are times when my heart aches for what I'll never have." He kissed the top of my head. "Never have someone to come home to. Never have the easiness of holding my partner's hand in public. Never have the chance to decide if we want children." He sighed deeply. "Never have someone to love me."

My heart squeezed and it was right on the tip of my tongue to spill my guts. *I want those same things. I want to be the one you come home to. Or maybe I want to come home to you. I want to be the one to love you. Could you ever love me?*

My stomach rolled. When had I ever wanted children? When had I ever even cared about holding hands with a guy in public? When had I ever been worried I'd never have someone to love me or someone to love?

All of the thoughts and feelings were strange and unfamiliar and I knew exactly when they'd started. Right about the time Jordan Moore took me to the river.

Damn Kingsley being so quiet and relaxed and good for me.

Damn Jordan for being so...well, for being so different and perfect and exactly what I wanted in my life. What I was beginning to think I *needed* in my life.

And damn the distance between us. I was a city boy through-and-through; I couldn't just up and leave my job. Jordan was a country boy born-and-bred; he belonged in Kingsley and would be miserable in the city. *City is city and country is country and never shall they meet* I thought sadly as my brain warped the old Kipling poem.

EIGHT

JORDAN

AND SO, it began.

I'd fallen for Marc—probably as far back as our night at the river—and, as much as I loved spending time with him, our time together was a heavy reminder of what I'd never have.

Marc was everything I'd ever wanted in a partner. He was drop-dead gorgeous, caring, fun to be around, and amazing in bed. But, more than that, he was intelligent, savvy, and a hard worker. He learned quickly, accepted challenges, and helped wherever asked. Yes, he often did all of those things with a sarcastic comment or a citified complaint nestled in, but it didn't make me love him any less.

Love.

Yeah, there was no denying it. I loved Marc Kingsley.

I loved my best friend's grandson.

I loved a person who was my exact opposite in so many ways.

I loved a man ten years my junior.

My heart pinched.

I loved a man who wanted nothing more than a three-month fling; a man who would high-tail it out of my country life at the end of his *sentence* and never look back.

And, just as I'd predicted, my heart was already breaking.

But, as Marc straddled my hips in the bed of my truck and stripped his t-shirt over his head, I forced myself to push aside the melancholy and enjoy the time we had left.

"Want you," he murmured against my lips as he leaned in for a soul-searing kiss.

"You've got me," I whispered and never before had words been so true.

In a flurry of arms and legs, lips and tongues, clothes and skin, we kissed and touched and undressed.

I yanked a long pillow from the pile and put it on the toolbox. "Kneel on there, lean on the cab," I ordered as I tossed a blanket to the roof of the truck for Marc to rest his elbows and chest.

"Been thinking about something," Marc began.

I cocked a brow and stroked myself slowly as I admired his gorgeous body. "As long as we were both tested and are monogamous for my time here, what do you say we skip the condoms?" He knelt before me and swallowed my cock as his eyes sparkled up at me in the moonlight.

I groaned. "I'm good with it; I trust you. No one else but you." In all honesty, I didn't see myself looking for hookups after Marc—at least not for a very long time—and I'd definitely get tested again if I ever found myself wanting that.

I ran my hand through his hair and fought the urge to fist his light brown locks and fuck hard and fast into his mouth. "Get on the toolbox and spread your legs."

Marc shivered as he climbed onto the toolbox and spread his legs wide as he leaned onto the cab of the truck. "Fuck, it's cold out here. Warm me up." He wiggled his perfect ass.

I knelt behind him and tongued his hole, loving the way he squirmed and whimpered as his muscle relaxed and opened for me. After I'd worked my finger and plenty of spit into him, I rustled in my jeans for a tiny packet of lube and smeared his entrance and my cock. Yeah, Marc being in my life had turned me into the type of man who carried lube packets in my pockets. And I didn't even care.

Aligning my head at his pucker, I leaned forward to cover his body and whispered gruffly in his ear, "Never done this with anyone else." Trusting someone enough to go without a condom was a huge deal for me and I needed Marc to know that.

I expected him to make a joke about never having sex in the bed of a truck after watching a movie on the side of a work shed. Instead, Marc took a shaky breath as his body opened for me. "Me neither. Never wanted to; no one I'd trust enough to do this with." His words caught in his throat. "Oh fuck, Jordan. Holy fuck that's so good."

His tight heat gripped me as I continued to sink deep into his ass. I was torn between wanting to slam my cock into him hard and fast and a deep longing to fuck him long and slow. Wanting this to last forever, I opted for long and slow.

In the quiet of the chilly spring night, with the moonlight casting a silver glow, I held Marc in my arms and made love to him. I wasn't supposed to fall in love with him. I definitely had no right to even consider telling him how I felt. But I could possibly show him with my body, with the way I held him, the way I stroked him, the way I slowly thrust into his ass and made his body come alive.

Marc turned his head and I captured his cries of pleasure with my lips as my tongue thrust in the same slow and deep rhythm as my throbbing cock.

"I want to feel you come in me," Marc murmured against my mouth. "Want to take your hot cum in my ass."

His words and the image they painted were enough to nearly send me over the edge and my thrusting hips faltered.

"Your ass is so hot and so tight; I want to come in you, feel my cum spill as your ass milks my cock."

Marc spread his legs even farther apart and groaned as I took turns stroking his hard length, fondling his balls, and caressing his taint. "Fuck, you're going to make me come doing that."

"Do it, come for me," I whispered against his ear. "Wanna feel your ass clenching around my dick as I unload in you."

"Next time, want you to fuck me on my back. Want to see you as you fuck me." Marc gasped. "Fuck if I've ever wanted that, but I want it with you."

The idea of Marc's legs spread open for me, his dick between us, our eyes meeting as my cock slid into his tight hole was more than I could handle. I wrapped both arms around his chest and pumped long and hard into him. "Jack yourself; come for me."

Marc fisted his cock and stroked three times before his strangled cry broke through the quiet night. "Fuuuuck, Jordan," he groaned.

As his ass clenched with his orgasm, I spilled in him with a slow moan and savored each hot spurt of my pulsing cock while I held Marc against my chest.

We rode out our releases together with a few more thrusts and groans, but all too soon, the cool air brought on shivers and I had to slip slowly from his body.

"Oh fuck, it's cold." Marc shifted on the toolbox. "Do we have a towel?" He held out his cum-covered hand.

I tossed him a pillow case. "We'll have to wash it."

Marc chuckled as he cleaned himself and handed the cloth to me. "Pretty sure the back window of your truck will also need cleaning. I'm guessing what I shot all over the glass isn't going to pass as bird shit."

I chuckled, threw the pillow case to the side, and grabbed

Marc to pull him to the mattress. I yanked the covers up to our shoulders and cuddled against his back.

"Holy shit, outside sex is exhausting," he mumbled. "Need to sleep. Then I need to wake up and ride you."

"Is that so?" I chuckled and kissed the top of his head.

"I mean, I'm in the country learning all of the country ways. I'd be remiss if I didn't take the chance to ride you like a rodeo horse in the bed of your truck."

"Seems like you're taking very well to the idea of experiencing all the country has to offer," I teased. Nipping at his neck and pressing my dick against his ass. "I'd be happy to play horse to your cowboy in the name of making sure you get an authentic country experience."

Marc wiggled his ass against me. "Give me a couple hours to sleep and you'll be calling me cowboy," he promised.

A couple hours later, Marc made good on his word as he rolled me to my back, straddled my hips, and took me into his cum-filled ass, and rode me for all he was worth before we both exploded with shouts of ecstasy.

"Explain to me once again what the point of fishing is," Marc grumbled as he swatted at a bug buzzing his face.

We'd driven to my favorite fishing spot, parked the truck, and were walking toward the hidden pond where I knew we'd catch plenty of bluegill. If Marc enjoyed the fishing experience, I'd take him to a spot where we could snag some catfish.

I smiled at the whine in Marc's question. "The point of fishing is to relax, enjoy yourself, and possibly catch fish that can be eaten as a meal. Ellie does an amazing job frying up fresh fish."

Marc wrinkled his nose. "I'm not against eating fish, but I kinda don't want to eat anything that can look at me."

"We don't *have* to keep them. We can toss them back. I'm sure Ellie will have so much food at the field party we won't even miss a mess of fried fish." I was thrilled that Marc and I were packing as much *country fun* into two days as possible.

We'd done all of our morning chores before fishing. Ellie and another neighbor were helping with a field party that evening. And Marc and I were going mushroom hunting the next day.

We'd spent every day of his first two months in Kingsley together and I was acutely aware that he was leaving in a month. I wanted to fill him up with as many memories of Kingsley as possible.

Selfishly—and possibly because I had a wish to torture myself—I also wanted to pack away as many memories of our time together as I could for myself.

Our daily routine had become the most fulfilling, easy, and enjoyable part of my life and my heart reminded me every minute of every day how much I'd break when he was gone.

But I still had thirty some days with him and I was determined to make the most of them. I suddenly had a bit more time to enjoy my time with him because Marc's plan for my business had taken hold and I'd recently been able to hire Ms. Bethany to help with the chickens and veggies, and Scott to help with most of the miscellaneous woodworking orders. The online orders had started pouring in and continued at a steady pace, and Marc had offered to keep the site updated for me even when he went back to Rockhurst.

Although part of me knew that the best way to get over him would be a clean break, I secretly clung to the knowledge that I'd maybe still have contact with him due to the website.

And Ellie.

But would I even be able to tell my best friend about my broken heart when it was her grandson I'd fallen in love with and who trampled all over my heart?

"Hey, where'd you go?" Marc's words penetrated the resigned fog of anxiety and anticipated heartbreak I'd let pull me under.

"Huh?" I glanced at him as we came to the edge of the water. "Oh, just thinking."

"Thinking about?" Marc set down the tackle box and fishing pole.

"Just that the business is going well and I'm glad I hired Ms. Bethany and Scott. They are really helpful."

"And?" Marc pushed.

I didn't want to bring the day down. We were supposed to enjoy our time together and build memories. Not get sad about the inevitable. But the way Marc wrapped his arms around my waist and pulled me close broke down all of my barriers.

Shrugging, I looped my arms around his neck. "Just thinking about how close we are to your three months being over. I knew time wouldn't stand still. I knew what I was getting into. But I'm not looking forward to the hurt. Going back to being alone and knowing what I'm missing without you in my life is going to suck."

Marc pressed his forehead to mine. "Two months ago, I never thought I'd be sad to leave this place. But now? After meeting you? It's going to be one of the hardest things I've ever done."

"But the break has been good for you, yeah? You're feeling better? Relaxed and recharged and ready to go back better than ever?" I ignored the part of my heart that begged me to ask him to stay, the part that wanted me to point out to him how great we were together, how good his life could be here. It wasn't my place.

"Kingsley has been amazing for my physical and mental health for sure. I'm ready to get back to work." He paused with a frown. "But not as excited about it as I'd thought I'd be."

"Why?"

"I guess I'm kinda worried I'll slip right back into the overworked, stressed, jumble of issues I was when I got sent here in the first place."

I brushed my lips over his. "Kingsley will always be here. Need a break? Need to rest and relax? We're only a couple hours away." *I'll always be here. Heartbroken, alone, waiting on the love of my life to return.* Damn, how pathetic did that make me sound?

"Rockhurst is only a couple hours from here. Maybe you could come visit from time-to-time?" Marc's eyes held an uncertainness I'd never seen before.

"What are you saying?" My words were barely a whisper.

"I'm saying that I want to enjoy our month, but I'm not one hundred percent sure that my going back to Rockhurst has to end *this*." He scowled. "I know we got into this knowing there was a time limit; I don't want to break the deal we had. I get it if you'd rather just stick to the plan. But..." He gestured between us. "We're good together, right?"

I nodded, my eyes and throat stinging. "But I'll be busy here, you'll be busy there. I have a real anxiety thing with the city. I'm not saying I'd refuse to come visit, but I can't promise I'd be any fun. And I couldn't do it often; I can't leave the farm. Kingsley is my home, my life."

Marc kissed me, slow and deep. "I'd never ask you to leave here. I didn't get it before, but I get it now. I see how Kingsley can get in a person's blood. But I'm willing to try the long-distance thing if you are."

"I've only ever heard of long-distance relationships not

working," I muttered. "And I don't know that I could be on board with you going back to your city hook-ups."

Marc frowned. "Who said I'd go back to those? A long-distance *relationship* would mean *you* and *me*. No one else."

"I'm willing to try it."

"But?" Marc asked.

"Just wondering if it's prolonging the inevitable. You'll get back to Rockhurst, settle back into your city life, and forget me. Either way, clean break or slow death, I'm left here nursing a broken heart, missing you, and longing for what I can't have."

"Shhh," Marc whispered against my ear. "We've got something good. I'm not ready to throw it away just because of a couple of hours drive between us. Let's enjoy our month and head into our separation as if it's just a bump in the road as we settle into the long-distance thing. I can't imagine Gran would let me get away with not coming to visit now that I've been living with her. We're not talking cross-country distance. I think we can make it work."

I blinked back tears. "I want to believe that. But I worry that city life will erase what we've had. And where do we stand in the long-run? Forever separated by two hours? Forever living separate lives? Only to meet up from time-to-time? What kind of life is that?"

Marc closed his eyes and sighed. "Honestly, I don't know. I just know that I feel something for you that I've *never* felt for anyone else and I'm not ready to give up on us." He feathered a kiss over my lips. "Can we just enjoy our time and promise we'll give it a chance even after I have to leave?"

I wanted to cling to Marc's words. *Have* to leave. Maybe he didn't want to go as much as I didn't want him to? Two months ago, he would have said *Get* to leave. Could I convince him to stay? Somehow show him that Kingsley was best for him?

No. I couldn't ask him to stay here. Just like he'd never ask me to leave Kingsley for him, I could never ask him to leave the life he'd built in Rockhurst for me.

Which brought us back to the crux of our problem.

"For now. I just want to spend time with you and try to forget you're leaving." It was a shitty way to deal, but it was all I felt strong enough for at that point.

Marc nodded and kissed me. "Well, you got me out here. I guess you better try to teach me to fish."

NINE

MARC

FIRST, no one told me I'd have to touch a damn worm to go fishing. Where were the fun fake worms and brightly colored fish toys? Okay, Jordan explained they were called *lures*, but whatever.

Look, I can deal with huge sales, angry clients, and stressful business issues. But worms? No. Maybe if I was starving and the only way I could eat was to put a squirming worm on a hook to catch a fish. But just for fun? No. No way.

Jordan baited my hook for me and taught me how to throw the line in the water. Okay, I think he called it *casting* the line. But I nearly *did* throw the whole thing in the water the first time.

We sat on the bank of a pond, watching our bobbers float in the still water, and chatted quietly. Pretty sure Jordan could have sat there for eight hours. Me? Not so much. The bugs were ridiculous. The fish just kept eating the worm off my hook—I guess it's a tasty treat for them?—and I was left with a bobber that would wobble a bit and then nothing.

Second, what the hell was happening to me? I came to

Kingsley under duress. I was forced to take a break. All I had to do was survive three months in a tiny country town with Gran and then I was home free to return to Rockhurst and my actual life.

Should have been easy.

Instead, I went and fell head over heels for Jordan Moore.

I glanced at the man next to me. He was sprawled in his chair, eyes closed as if he was completely relaxed. There was absolutely zero about the guy that I would have ever thought I could fall for. And yet, there I was, loving absolutely everything about him. Yeah, I said the L-word. The thought of it nearly made me hyperventilate, but there was no denying it.

Jordan was drop-dead gorgeous, creative, a hard worker, and such a good-hearted person. He was the most amazing lover I'd ever had—the fact that I *only* thought of having sex with him and no one else—like in a forever way; oh God, I was so screwed—was a huge deal for me—but more than that, I just loved spending time with him. I loved that he took time to teach me things. I loved his sense of humor. I loved the way he treated people. And I loved how dedicated he was to his farm; it wasn't just that he felt a sense of loyalty—although, he did—it was that he truly adored Kingsley and he didn't need anything big or flashy. I loved his heart.

And I had to leave him.

Which would break that heart I loved so much.

I hated it.

But my job was in Rockhurst.

My *life* was in Rockhurst.

The city was in me as much as the country was in Jordan.

But the last sixty days had made me think that maybe I could split my time between the two. Maybe. I loved

Kingsley. But Rockhurst was my home; I'd built a life there and I couldn't just throw it away.

Could I?

Jordan finally had mercy on me when I yelped at a bee buzzing my head. He chuckled and said we could pack up and head home. I nearly toppled my chair as I shot up and started gathering our stuff.

As we walked toward the truck—I'd truly never again see a truck like Jordan's without thinking of the amazing sex we'd had in it—I took Jordan's hand.

"So, is fishing always so exciting and fun?" I teased.

"Today wasn't the best; but sometimes it's good to just sit and think. Enjoy the sun and the sounds of nature."

"Oh, you mean the bug noises—like the huge bee that buzzed my head trying to attack me? That's the only real sound I heard."

Jordan snorted. "You weren't listening hard enough. Frogs, birds, the wind, they all combine to make a gorgeous song."

I dropped the tackle box and chair I was carrying and shoved Jordan against a tree. His mouth opened on a gasp and I teased and tasted while rocking my hips against his. When we finally broke apart, I whispered, "I adore the way you love this place. I'm so grateful I got to know Kingsley through your eyes."

Jordan licked his lips and swallowed. "And I adore watching you fall in love with my home—even if it's just a tiny bit here and there before you go."

~

"WAIT, I think maybe our definition of *party* is very different," I said as I stood in the middle of an open field. "This looks like an empty field."

Jordan laughed. "Field parties are a country staple. Take a field that's left fallow or an open pasture—hell, even just a big back yard—and you've got your perfect location."

"For what? Boring yourself to death?" I wrinkled my nose as I glanced around the space. "It's just an empty piece of land."

"Now it is, sure. But we'll get that bonfire going, people will pull their trucks and ATV's up, there will be food, drinks, and music. A party of epic proportions." Jordan lowered the tailgate of his truck and pulled a table out of the bed and began to set it up.

"*Epic*? There's not even electricity."

Jordan shook his head with a scoffing chuckle. "Oh, ye of little faith. Just wait."

"What's this party even for?"

"This one is to celebrate the beginning of the BnB season. But field parties can happen for any reason. Graduation, weddings, bachelor parties, anniversaries, just an excuse to drink; you name it, a field party can cover it."

Ninety minutes later, I had to admit I'd been wrong. Nearly fifty vehicles had pulled into the field and formed a sort of stacked ring of circles around the bonfire. People piled from their cars, trucks, and ATV's with tables, chairs, coolers, and food.

A truck hauling a trailer pulled up and within forty-five minutes, a whole stage and band were set up—complete with speakers, so clearly, they'd found a way to bring electricity to the field—and a mixture of old rock and a wide variety of country began to fill the field as the sun sank lower and lower on the horizon.

There was seriously enough food to feed a damn army. Beer and liquor flowed freely. And the people in attendance truly seemed to be enjoying themselves.

Gran introduced me to several of her friends and people

from town. I found myself answering all sorts of questions about *the big city*. I smiled and made polite conversation—I was a successful businessman for a reason, after all—but all I really wanted to do was find Jordan, wrap my arms around him, and have him teach me how to roast a marshmallow.

I froze.

Damn it.

Jordan wasn't out to most of the town. Gran knew. Others probably had suspicions. But I couldn't just find him in a crowd of townsfolk and put my hands all over him. I was leaving; Jordan lived here. I would never force him out before he felt ready.

"Hey, Oxford, you ready to experience the awesomeness that is a fire-roasted marshmallow?" Jordan spoke easily from my side as he greeted the people I was talking to. "Sorry, y'all. I've promised to show the city boy all the best of a country field party; we've got to go roast a few marshmallows."

We left the little crowd and headed toward the fire.

"Teach me, oh wise one," I teased as I nudged him with my elbow. "Gotta say," I lowered my voice when we were away from listening ears, "not being able to touch you or just be *us* is killing me right now." And how unfair of me was that? I had no right to put pressure on him. "Sorry, that wasn't fair. Just miss the easy way when we're not around people."

Jordan threw a sad glance my way. "I miss it, too. But this is my life, it's just the way things are."

I looked around at all the people visiting, laughing, eating, and even a few who were dancing. "I don't know. I'd never out you or push you on something you're not ready for, but," I shrugged, "I really don't know that many people would care."

"Or they'd care and I'd lose business." Jordan picked up a

bag of marshmallows and two long metal items that looked like gigantic forks. I recognized them as tools used to roast hot dogs over a fire.

"Not many people sell eggs, fryers, or veggies around here; would so many folks really be able to withhold their business?" I gestured toward the crowd. "And even if you did lose a few, would it be enough to make a negative impact? Probably not now that your woodworking business is going strong."

Jordan's face clouded with what appeared to be a mixture of regret and anger. "What does it even matter? There's no real reason to out myself. The people who really matter already know. Once you leave, I'm back to being alone. No reason to bring unnecessary attention on myself or potentially lose business when I have no one to go out with. If you were here for good, I'd likely do it in a heartbeat," he paused and pressed his lips together, "well, at least somewhat quicker. But I won't have you around to hold hands with, go to dinner with, attend field parties with. If we were truly together, I'd want to be able to be a real couple." He shrugged. "As it is, you're leaving and I'll soon be back to being by myself. No need to rock the boat or invite trouble."

My heart squeezed. If I was staying in Kingsley, Jordan would come out and make it clear we were a real couple? Why did I want that so badly? When had I ever wanted a man to claim me as his? Why did I want Jordan to come out and show off his partner, but only if it was *me*?

I was a selfish ass. "I'm sorry. You have to do what's best for you. It's not right of me to push you." I stood as close to him as I could without actually touching. "Just know I support you no matter what. Way out here in the country or from the big city; I just want you to be happy."

"And yet, we both know I'm very soon not going to be,"

Jordan mumbled so low I wasn't completely sure I caught what he said. "Let's do these marshmallows."

Five minutes later, we were laughing as my marshmallow burned to charcoal.

"Okay, I think you need to focus more on keeping it close to the heat, but not close enough it can catch fire." Jordan used his metal stick to knock the flaming chunk of sugar into the fire. He handed me another marshmallow. "Try again."

Afraid of burning it again, I took forever and the soft candy was barely warm when I tested it. "How do I suck at this? It's burning sugar, how can I mess that up?"

"To be fair," Jordan drawled, "you actually did quite well with *burning* the sugar. You need to work on toasting the sugar." He removed a perfectly toasted marshmallow from the fire and held it out to me. "Pull it off; careful, it's hot."

I popped the browned sugar cube into my mouth and groaned. The outer shell was perfectly golden and crispy while the inside was soft and gooey. "That's so not fair. I want to make one that good."

We spent several more minutes roasting marshmallows. I never actually achieved a perfect one, but I got close. And my stomach was beginning to protest all of the samples I'd eaten during the process.

"Boys, can you come help me at the house?" Gran asked.

Jordan and I cleaned up—well, the best one can clean up in the middle of a field—and followed her from the fire.

When we reached the pond, away from the crowd and lit only by the bonfire and moonlight, Gran faced us. "I wasn't going to say anything, but watching you two tonight, I just can't keep quiet."

My heart jumped to my throat and I wanted more than anything to glance toward Jordan, but I did my best to keep my cool. "What's wrong?"

"Nothing's *wrong* per se. But I need you both to know that

I'm one hundred percent in support of you. I'm torn between knowing you're both going to get hurt and hoping that something amazing comes from this even if it gets rocky before it gets better."

"I'm not sure I completely understand," I started to deny, but Gran and Jordan both snorted.

"How long have you known?" Jordan asked.

"About six weeks for sure. You two may think you're sly, but the attraction and connection are almost like an aura around you." Gran reached out and patted us both on the shoulder. "At first, I was slightly concerned. The age issue, the fact that it's my grandson and my best friend, and what the end of three months was going to bring."

"And now?" I asked.

"Now, my only concern is the end of the three months. The age difference is nothing. And I'd be crazy not to want my grandson and best friend as happy as the two of you make each other."

"Well, that makes two of us," Jordan muttered. "But we knew our time was limited when we decided to do this."

"We may try the long-distance thing," I offered weakly.

"I want nothing more than for you boys to find your forever together; I want you both happy." Gran's eyes twinkled in the moonlight.

"But?" Jordan asked.

"No *but*," Gran quipped. "Just enjoy your time and don't fight fate and where it leads you." She glanced toward the fire and the crowd. "You're welcome to come back to the party, but I completely understand if you want to duck out and spend your night together. Be sure to come over for breakfast before you leave for mushroom hunting tomorrow."

That was how Jordan and I found ourselves wandering to the side of the barn where he'd parked his truck after unloading it. Part of me felt guilty for leaving the party, but

I'd seen a field party and truly just wanted to spend my time with Jordan.

"Are you surprised she knew?" I asked.

Jordan shrugged as he started the truck. "Not really. She knows me well. She's very perceptive. And she knows you. I'm kinda relieved to not have to hide it."

"But?"

"But it doesn't change that you're leaving. Doesn't make it any easier." Jordan pointed the truck toward his house.

I watched the darkness glide by the window, lost in my own thoughts of leaving.

When we pulled into the driveway, Jordan parked the truck and lead the way to the house. "Shower?"

"Definitely, I feel smoky from the fire." I threw my arms around Jordan and laughed when he bent low to give me a ride on his back. "And then I want to spend the rest of this night in bed."

"Need to be up and getting chores done early so we can head out to the woods for mushroom hunting, but we've got all night." Jordan dropped me at the bathroom door. "Go ahead and take your time. Holler at me when you're ready for me to join."

I cocked my head to the side, always appreciative of his understanding that I'd need a little time to myself before sex. "You know, I'm still very interested in topping. If you're still interested?"

Jordan's nostrils flared. "Interested? Definitely, yes. But I'm a bit afraid it would make losing you even harder. Can't miss something I've not experienced, right?"

I bit my lip and reached out to caress his chest. "I don't know. I've never had my dick deep in your ass, but I'm pretty sure I already miss it."

Jordan growled and leaned in for a lip-tingling, magical kiss that spoke volumes of promises for later. "Well, I'm missing *my* dick deep in *your* ass, so go get yourself ready."

After a quick prep, I jumped into the shower and hollered at Jordan as the showerhead rained down on me, while I lathered with shampoo and body wash.

Jordan joined me and took a quick turn at washing all the important parts and pieces before he wrapped his arms around me.

I buried my face in his neck. "Wanna rim you and make you come. Then later, you can fuck me."

He groaned and rocked his hot cock against mine. "No complaints here."

I dropped to my knees and took his long, thick cock between my lips and hummed when he moaned and thrust deep. I loved sucking him off, but I wanted more. "Turn around," I commanded.

Jordan turned and faced the tile wall. I stood for a moment and wedged my hard shaft between the perfect, round globes of his ass. "Not gonna lie, really wanna slide my dick deep inside you." I smiled against his ear when he thrust his hips back. "I'll respect your wishes, but you're still gonna come for me with either my tongue or fingers in your ass."

He shivered in my arms before I nudged his legs apart.

"Spread your legs and give me that pretty hole."

Jordan widened his stance and bent slightly.

I pulled his cheeks apart and teased the tight pucker with my wet finger before leaning in and swirling my tongue over his hole.

Jordan groaned and shoved his ass back like he wanted me to keep my face buried there.

I reached around and took his throbbing cock in my hand and began to stroke as I tongued his ass. When Jordan's body trembled, I stood, plastered to his side, as I kissed him, never taking my hand from his dick. "Gonna fuck you with my fingers," I whispered against his mouth. I slid my other hand down his back and pressed at his entrance with my wet finger.

Jordan tensed when I breached him, but I never stopped jacking his shaft and deepened the kiss. When I added a second finger, I knew from the way his hips thrust and his tongue tangled with mine that he was close. "Come for me," I said gruffly against his ear. "Wanna feel your ass hug my fingers as your cock spills all over my hand."

Jordan pumped his hips and a deep growl filled the shower stall as his orgasm overtook him. His tight ring clenched around my fingers and his shaft throbbed as spurts of cum coated my fist.

We stayed in the shower—just holding each other—until the water ran cold.

"Fuck, I feel like my bones just ran down the drain after that," Jordan mumbled. "You may have to settle for a blow job if I can't get it up again."

I tossed him a towel. "Or you can blow me *now* and we'll both rest up for a second round."

Jordan growled and hustled me toward the bed. He climbed on and laid in the middle. "Straddle my chest and fuck my mouth the way you want to fuck my ass," he ordered.

My cock—which had been begging to come since the shower—jerked as precum beaded on the tip. I dropped the towel and launched myself onto the bed, straddled Jordan's chest, and moaned as my balls pressed against his hot, damp skin. Taking my hard shaft in hand, I tapped the head against his lips. "Open up."

Jordan licked his lips, his tongue brushing over my sensitive head. His lips parted as his fiery eyes stared up at me.

I fed my cock between his lips and groaned as his wet

heat took me deep. Jordan had said to fuck his mouth the way I wanted to fuck his ass. But that was a conundrum because I was torn in that aspect. Part of me wanted to fuck him hard and fast, but I also dreamed of taking him long and slow. Deciding to just enjoy however it ended up working out, I shifted to hold onto the headboard and lifted my hips so I could thrust into his mouth. The image of Jordan spread before me, face-down, as I fucked into his ass filled my head. I growled and continued pumping my hips as his lips stretched around me.

Jordan, knowing how much I loved my balls played with, cupped my heavy sac in one hand and reached to stroke himself.

"Don't come yet. Your next one's going to be inside me." I increased my pace and threw my head back as Jordan continued to tease my balls. My orgasm built with each thrust and, within moments, I gave one last pump of my hips as my cock exploded into Jordan's greedy mouth.

After riding out my release, I pulled from his mouth, let go of the headboard, and collapsed onto Jordan as I savored the blissed out feeling that washed over me. "Holy fuck, think of how great that will be when you let me top."

Jordan mumbled from under me.

"What was that?" I asked.

He pushed me off him. "I said I didn't want to suffocate before the next round. Your dead weight was blocking my airway."

"And here I thought choking on my cock would be the way to go," I teased.

Jordan snorted as he took me in his arms. "Give me a few and I'll be ready."

～

I WOKE a couple hours later to Jordan's lips against my ear and his cock pressed against my ass. "You ready?"

I groaned, rolled to my back, and spread my legs.

Jordan's face registered the briefest surprise, but he settled on top of me and rocked his hips, rutting his cock against mine. He wrapped his arms around me and devoured my mouth; the man's kisses never got old and never failed to send electric charges through my body. "I want to take you this way," he whispered against my lips.

Two months ago, I *never* would have wanted sex in such an intimate position. But now? The image of watching Jordan's face as he entered me danced through my head and I knew I wanted exactly what he was asking for. I nodded and pushed my hips up. "Wanna watch you as you fuck me."

Jordan kissed me, our tongues dancing in a hot and sweet prelude of what was to come. Breaking from my mouth, he pressed kisses down my chest before reaching for the lube bottle and tossing it on the bed. Dipping his tongue into my slit, trailing his lips down my throbbing cock, he made his way to my balls before pushing my hips up and spreading my ass. I whimpered as his tongue dipped and teased, tasted and swirled, against my hole.

Once he had me good and wet, Jordan grabbed the lube. On his knees, his rock-hard shaft bobbing proudly from a neatly trimmed thatch of dark hair, Jordan slicked himself before shifting on top of me and pressing his cock head against my well-rimmed entrance.

As Jordan's thick head inched in, breaching my tight muscle, I reveled in the glorious sensations of watching his face and feeling my body stretch open for his invasion. Jordan's nostrils flared and his dark eyes flashed. I panted as I took him deeper and deeper, his hot, wide cock nearly taking my breath. The intimacy of our position most definitely knocking the wind from me.

With my legs spread wide, Jordan's balls pressed against my ass, and my leaking cock smearing precum all over my stomach, I reached for him and pulled him to my chest for a deep kiss. No kisses, no sex, had ever been like it was with Jordan. My body was lit on fire, my heart nearly pounded from my chest, and my thoughts ran through crazy ideas like marriage and forever.

Jordan wrapped me in his arms and pumped long and slow into me as he kissed me. I knew—maybe because I loved him too—that he was pouring every ounce of his love into me. And my heart simultaneously soared and broke. How could I leave what I'd found in Jordan?

Could we make long distance work?

Jordan's abdomen rubbed against my cock with each thrust into my ass and my balls drew tight. "Gonna come," I groaned.

Jordan increased his speed, holding me tighter, his hot breath against my neck. "Come for me, wanna feel your ass squeeze around me."

My cock exploded, painting my sticky release between our bodies. "Fuuuck, come in me. Give me your cum." I was addicted to feeling Jordan bare in me, knowing I was the only one he'd ever shared that with. No other man would ever satisfy me the way Jordan did; I'd never trust anyone to take me in this way.

His arms trembled around me as he let out a low growl. His cock throbbed as he pulsed his release into me.

We stayed plastered together, our bodies enjoying aftershocks for several moments. All too soon, Jordan's spent cock slid from my body. He grabbed a towel from the floor, cleaned himself, and wiped my belly and ass. He pulled me close and kissed the side of my head. "I don't mean to make our situation any worse than it already is, but I need to tell you something."

I tensed. "Worse? I don't see what we have as bad."

"No matter what, you're leaving. And what I need to tell you will make it harder."

I waited.

Jordan sighed. "Marc, I love you. I'm *in* love with you. And this is so much harder than I ever could have imagined it being."

Tears stung my eyes, but I blinked them away. "I love you, too. I think I have for almost my whole time here." I rolled to face him. "I really thought that falling in love for the first time would throw me for a loop in a negative way, but with you it just came so naturally that it seemed like there was no way around it." I caressed his cheek. "Maybe it will make it harder to leave, but I see it differently. We love each other; there's no doubt about that. That should make it easier to make long-distance work. We've got something special. We want to make it work—or at least, *I* want to. We'll figure it out."

"Of course, I want the same, but neither of us can give up our lives. No matter what, we're facing a forever of living apart. What kind of relationship is that?"

I swallowed thickly. "Are you interested in someone else —if you found a man who could give up his life and be here in Kingsley with you—would you want that?"

Jordan shook his head, his chin rubbing against the top of my head. "Before you? Yes. Very much. After you? Even if what we have can't survive long-distance, I don't see me ever finding someone else. You've ruined me for anyone else."

"Same for me. Before you, I wasn't at all interested in a forever relationship. If you and I don't work, I won't be looking elsewhere. But what we have? I'm willing to work for it; I want to put forth the effort."

"I guess I just need to adjust to living apart and seeing

you only once in a while," Jordan whispered. "Just going to miss you so damn bad."

"I know," I mumbled against his chest. "At least we're a pretty easy drive away and we have technology to keep in touch. I think we can make it work."

Jordan nodded and held me even tighter. "Sleep. Tomorrow is mushroom hunting."

TEN

JORDAN

"Okay, I will admit I haven't given much thought to mushroom hunting," Marc muttered, almost as if concerned, as we finished up our morning chores.

The hot house gardens were still producing well, and the outside gardens were growing at exactly the right pace. I expected the plants to set on vegetables within two or three weeks. The strawberries were planted late, so they'd be the last ready to pick.

I wondered often if Marc would be around long enough for him to help harvest any of the veggies from the larger outside gardens. And I imagined I'd come to see the strawberries in a bittersweet way as they'd be a season-long memory of Marc.

"But you're now giving mushroom hunting a lot of thought?" I bumped my hip against his as we entered the chicken coop.

"I'm just not sure it's a great activity for me," Marc began, running a hand through his hair before he grabbed a basket for eggs. He reached into his pocket and fished out the little packet of dried meal worms he'd bought the last time we were at the feed store. The chickens came rushing toward him.

My heart warmed even as it nearly strangled itself with sadness. Two months ago, Marc would have freaked out and run from them. But now? He put the basket to the side and poured the dried worms into his hand. Wordlessly, he handed the bag to me, shared the worms equally between both hands, and knelt down to let the chickens gobble up the special treat as he chuckled.

"If you're completely against it, we don't have to go," I said.

He held his hand out for more and gave the birds more of their yummy snack. "It's just that I'm not really all that into guns. I'm kinda worried I won't be much fun; I really don't even want to hold a gun let alone actually *shoot* mushrooms." He cocked his head. "But now that I say that out loud it doesn't even make sense. Mushrooms are alive in that they are living, but why do they need to be shot?"

I stared at him for several moments, blinking rapidly. *Jordan, do not laugh. Do not laugh at him and make him feel bad. Keep a straight face. Oh my God, he is so fucking adorable.* I cleared my throat. "Oh, um. There's maybe been a bit of a misunderstanding. Mushroom hunting doesn't actually involve *hunting* as in with guns. We just go hunting for them as in looking for them. It's kinda like a hide-n-seek type thing. They aren't always easy to find."

Marc's eyes went wide as he stood and brushed his hands on his pants before he hung his head. "Oh my God, I'm a complete idiot. See, this is exactly why I belong in the city." He shook his head. "I seriously thought you were going to have me shoot little defenseless mushrooms."

I threw my arm around his shoulder. "You're not an idiot. You've never lived in an area where mushroom hunting was something people did. It's logical that you wouldn't know what it involved."

Marc cuddled into my embrace. "I feel dumb."

"No, don't. If anything, I appreciate that you'd speak up. If something I planned for us to do made you uncomfortable, I'd want to know. I have my father's guns, but I don't really go hunting or use guns often. I know how to handle them, use them, clean them safely. But I'm not a huge gun enthusiast." I kissed the top of his head. "So, no guns involved in mushroom hunting. You still want to go?"

His cheeks flushed pink, but Marc nodded. "Yeah. Let's get food from Gran and then we can head out."

I wasn't sure if Marc would ever be able to laugh at the misunderstanding, but it would forever be a memory I'd cherish as an example of why I loved him so much.

And a memory of what you lost and what you'll never have again my heart nagged.

Two hours later, after we'd finished chores, visited with Ellie while picking up food she wanted us to take, and driven to my favorite mushroom hunting spot, we climbed from the truck.

The day was perfect for finding morels. The day before had seen rain and the ground was slightly damp, but the morning was warm and muggy. I tossed Marc a brown paper bag.

"What am I even looking for?" Marc wrinkled his nose.

I opened my phone and showed him a few pictures of morels I'd found in the past.

"I don't get how those are hard to find."

"Well, sometimes they are found in huge amounts. Sometimes you only find one or two. Often if there's one, look around because there are more. They blend in really well." I lead the way into the woods.

"What do we *do* with them once we find them?" Marc asked from behind me.

"If we find enough, we'll fry them up. The grocer pays for morels by the pound. If we find a large amount, we could sell to him or let neighbors know we have some for sale." I held a branch aside so Marc could walk through.

"They're really that good?"

"A real treat out here. I'm sure you can cook them other ways, but finding a mess of mushrooms and frying them up is as country as it gets." My eyes scanned the ground as we walked. I really hoped we found a large mess of the little things.

"Well then, I guess it's a requirement since I'm trying to do all things country."

About five minutes of walking into the woods, we found a spot where a large tree had fallen and began to rot. The ground was covered in leaves and dappled sunlight.

And then I saw it.

A perfect little morel. And there were three more next to it.

"I found some. But I want you to find them." I gestured toward the general area.

Marc moved closer to the dead tree and squinted his eyes. "I don't see them. Are the damn things wearing camo? You know how I feel about camo. Why can't they have little neon signs to let me know where they are?" He continued to grumble for several moments until finally he gasped. "Oh my God! I see one!" He knelt down and touched it. "Do I just pull it from the ground?"

I nodded. "But there's more than one." I nodded toward the others.

"Oh!" Marc grabbed all four mushrooms and placed them gently into his bag.

From that point on, Marc and I could barely keep up with

picking the morels. I wasn't sure if I'd ever found so many in one trip. We easily filled both of our large bags.

"We should probably leave some for others to find." I wiped a hand over my brow. "Plus, I'm hot, tired, and hungry. Let's get in the air conditioning and eat what Ellie sent."

Marc beamed as he carried his full bag plastered against his chest. "That was so much fun. I'd definitely give it a ten out of ten."

I laughed. "Well, you must be a good luck charm because I've *never* found that many all at once. That was amazing." I took the bag from him and put them both in the bed of the truck securely under the tool box. "It's not always that fun."

"Well, you've spoiled me. I'll expect to fill two grocery bags every time from here on out." Marc kissed me. "Thank you. I've really enjoyed learning the ways of a true country boy."

We climbed into the truck and I blasted the air conditioning. "You wanna take our food to the river?"

Fire flashed in Marc's eyes. "Our river?"

My gut twisted. *Our river.* Another part of my life that would forever be wrapped up in my memories of our time together. "Yeah, our river. Just another spot."

"Sounds perfect."

I headed the truck toward the river.

"Thank God your truck has air conditioning." Marc gave a groan and stuck his face right in front of the air vent.

"It's not even summertime hot yet," I teased. "Just you wait."

A look passed between us as if we both realized at the same time that Marc wouldn't be in Kingsley during the hottest part of the summer.

He sighed and let the cool air blow on his face. "How did people live before air conditioning?"

I chuckled. "I guess you can't miss what you've not experienced."

Marc turned suggestive eyes my way. "So I've been told," he said gruffly.

I knew immediately he was referring to when I said the same about bottoming for him.

I swallowed thickly.

"I don't mean to pressure you. You have to be the one to make the decision. I'm perfectly happy bottoming, but I don't want you missing out on something you want."

I shrugged. "Just feels like it would make me miss what we have even more when it inevitably doesn't work out."

Marc grumbled. "Why do you insist that it won't work out? We're just over two hours apart. We'll see each other often. We'll talk daily. We'll take turns visiting each other."

I took a deep breath. "I want more than a partner I get to *visit* from time-to-time."

Marc frowned. "I thought you said you didn't want anyone but me."

"I don't," I insisted. "I'm just saying that I've never dreamed of finding a man I get to see *from time-to-time*. And what happens when your work takes over? Lunch phone calls get canceled because of business lunch meetings. Nighttime video chats get pushed off because of your work load. Visits to Kingsley get cut short because of work back in Rockhurst. Even if we could plan a trip somewhere together, there's every possibility that your work will interfere." I clenched the steering wheel. "And even if I overcome my anxiety about the city, I can't leave the farm for weeks at a time. I'm up earlier than Rockhurst you. I'm in bed earlier than Rockhurst you." I turned a pained look toward Marc and hated the sadness on his face. "We can try it. I want it to work more than anything. But I have to be realistic. There's a very real possibility that it won't work no matter how badly we want it to."

He nodded. "I understand that." Marc reached for my hand. "But I feel like we met for a reason; it's like we both needed each other. Before you, I would have scoffed at *meant to be* or *fate* or whatever. But now? There's no denying it. We have something special. I know this because I've been with more than my fair share of men and *never* felt this—not even an inkling—with anyone else. Maybe it's different for you…"

"No. Not even close. I'm sure I could find someone to be at least somewhat compatible with. Maybe set up a comfortable life with him. But the spark that burns between us isn't something I'll ever find with anyone else." I gritted my teeth in hopes of stopping the tears that wanted to fill my eyes. "That's why losing you will wreck me."

"Then we don't lose each other."

I shook my head with a huff. "Maybe it's because you're so much younger, and I *do* appreciate your optimism, but plans don't always work, dreams don't always come true."

"Nope. I won't accept that." Marc squeezed my hand. "I've faced large boardrooms of intimidating people. I've made *the* sale in huge, stressful situations. I'm not giving up without a fight."

"I can see how your determination serves you well in your business." I gave him a wry smile. "I'm not sure belligerence is as useful in a real-life romance situation." I pulled the truck onto a dirt road that I knew would lead to the river. I wasn't taking him to an area where people were likely to be; I wanted to spend our time alone.

Once we drove as close to the river as I could get the truck, I parked under a large tree.

"Wow, we're so close. This is a lot different than that first night. No bluff here?" Marc asked as he gazed wide-eyed around the gorgeous river bank.

"Nope. The bluff starts a few miles north. There's one south of here, too." I gestured to the right and left. "There are some areas of the river here in Kingsley that are *right on* the river's edge—they flood terribly when the river is high—but most are a bit higher than this spot."

Marc shot a look toward the river. "We're okay here? It's not going to flood?"

I smiled patiently. "No, there's been rain lately, but not enough to flood the river. But you can totally see where the flood waters go." I pointed toward the grove of trees to the right and then nodded my head toward the large tree we parked under.

Marc's eyes went wide. "Whoa, for real?" He climbed from the truck and wandered to the front end.

I smiled as I took in the man before me. No longer *Oxford*, except when I wanted to tease him—and once he returned to the city. He looked completely at home in his work jeans, well-fitted t-shirt, work boots, and a ball cap turned backwards on his head.

Marc stood with his hands on his hips as he scanned the area.

I got out of the truck and joined him.

"You're telling me that those lines on the trees are where the water reaches when it floods?" He pointed to the trees.

"Yep. That lower one," I pointed to the grove, "is likely where the last flood reached. It wasn't very high at all and receded quickly." I turned to the big tree we stood next to. "This one is amazing to me."

Marc turned and his eyes traveled from the large gnarly roots up the trunk with a whistle. "No way." His head whipped to look at me. "I can see different lines, but you *can't* tell me that red line means what I think it means."

I smiled with a nod. "Yep. That was a flood of epic proportions; definitely part of Kingsley's history. Never seen one like it since then. I was just a little kid, but I remember it devastated the riverfront and a lot of the town. Hope to never see it get that bad again."

Marc frowned. "But doesn't a tree grow? Surely the red paint line has gotten higher over the years as the tree has grown."

I shook my head and moved to wrap my arms around Marc's waist. I leaned my chin on his shoulder. "Little known fact for a lot of people, a tree does get taller for several years. But once a tree reaches about one hundred and fifty years old, it simply gets wider and adds more rings without adding height. It may grow for another one hundred years, but it will only add rings not height."

Marc murmured, "Wow, that's kinda amazing."

"Which part?" I pressed a kiss under his ear and then brushed my lips against his cheek.

"All of it. I didn't know that about trees." His gaze slid up the tree again. "It's crazy to think this tree was here over one hundred and fifty years ago." He shook his head. "And even crazier to think that water *ever* reached that high. I can't imagine the level of disaster that brought to Kingsley."

"Took several years to recover. But we weren't the only town affected. Pretty much every river town had destruction from the water. The farther down the river, the worse the flooding. Kingsley was somewhere in the middle as far as how bad we got it."

"I need to ask Gran and Gramps for more Kingsley stories." He leaned his head against mine. "I feel like I've missed a lot of important things regarding their life and this place because it didn't affect me. How much of a selfish prick can I be?" he scoffed.

"Nah, you didn't have any connection to the town so it didn't register with you. Now that you have a connection it's more interesting." I ran my hands up and down his chest.

"We can go to the library to read some of their historical pieces sometime if you want."

Marc groaned as my knuckles traveled lower to brush over his zipper. "Mmm, sounds good. But right now, I want to eat and then maybe we have some playtime?"

"Perfect plan," I growled in his ear.

"Are you going to tease me if I say I'd rather have a little picnic in the air-conditioned truck than in the sticky air riddled with bugs and the smell of river?"

A laugh bubbled from my chest. "No, Oxford. I expected nothing less."

He shot me a glare, but happily climbed into the truck and pointed two of the vent fans toward his face. "Seriously, why does it feel so much hotter here? It's not like Rockhurst is in a different climate zone than Kingsley."

I grabbed the basket Ellie had packed for us and moved my seat back as far as it would go. "It's likely pretty much the same, but I doubt you spend a lot of time outdoors back in the city."

Marc copied the move with his seat as I rustled through the ice packs to pull six containers from the basket along with two plates, two cups, and two sets of silverware wrapped in napkins. The last large item was a thermos of what I assumed was tea. I peered into the basket to see that Ellie had even packed little packets of salt, pepper, and sweetener. Which meant the tea was unsweet. Which meant Ellie had given in to Marc's hatred of our Kingsley staple drink. I rolled my eyes at what that man could get people to do. Oh well, easier to sweeten mine with a packet than to unsweeten his. If unsweet tea meant Marc would stay, I'd drink it by the gallon.

"Yeah, that's true. I'm basically only outside to walk to and from my apartment, car, and office, and maybe a quick jaunt down the block for food. I usually have lunch delivered at work and dinner delivered at my apartment." He grabbed a plate, a cup, and silverware.

Did Marc ever notice that he most commonly referred to his place of residence as *the apartment* or *my apartment* and almost never as his *home*? I forced myself not to read too much into that.

Climbing from the truck, I discarded the basket in the truck bed until we needed it again. "You sure you don't want a sweet picnic on a blanket by the river edge?" I knew for a fact Marc did *not* want that, but I couldn't help but tease him.

"Nope. This is perfect," he said with a smile. "But get in, you're letting out the cold air."

Balancing plates on our knees, we filled them with Ellie's amazing pasta salad—which no matter how many times she assured me I was following the recipe correctly always tasted ten times better than mine—hot house tomatoes and cottage cheese, and bread and butter with strawberry jam.

After doctoring our tomatoes and cottage cheese with salt and pepper, smearing creamy butter and strawberry jam on our bread, and pouring ourselves each a cup of tea, we were ready to eat.

"Bet you'd never get *this* kind of meal delivered in Rockhurst," I said around a bite of pasta salad.

"No way," Marc agreed. "Although, until I came here, I wouldn't even have considered this a meal. But I'll be so full after this I won't be ready to eat until we get a late dinner ready—and even then, I doubt I'll be starving."

"This is the type of food that folks describe as *stick to your ribs*," I offered. "When the farmers are out in the fields or tending their livestock, they don't have time to be stopping for food. Breakfast and lunch need to keep them full."

"I honestly would have thought I'd gain weight eating all the carbs and fat, but I guess I'm so busy and active working at your place and the BnB that it balances out." Marc took a bite of tomato and cottage cheese and moaned. "This should be disgusting, but it's so damn good. *How* does a tomato grown out here taste so much better than one I can get at the store?"

"Hot house tomatoes may not match the superb flavor of a summer grown tomato, but home grown and fresh is always better than anything you can get in a store." I took a bite of tomato; it really was delicious.

"Summer tomatoes are going to be better than *this*?" Marc's eyes went wide and he paused chewing. "Okay, I've *got* to make plans to come back for tomatoes *and* strawberries at least."

"Just for those things, huh?" I teased.

"Well, food-wise, yes. And maybe some corn on the cob and bread and gravy. But outside of food, I'm pretty sure a certain chicken and veggie farmer's bed may lure me back to Kingsley as well."

I stirred packets of sweetener into my tea as Marc savored his bread with butter and strawberry jam.

"I'm absolutely ruined for store-bought bread, margarine, and manufactured strawberry jelly," he said as he finished the bread and took a final bite of pasta salad. Then he sniffed his tea. "Did you just add *more* sugar to your tea or is this regular, non-syrup tea?"

I laughed. "It's plain ol' tea. Seems like you convinced Ellie to cater to your snobbish ways."

"Hey, just because I don't like my tea to mirror high fructose corn syrup in both consistency and sweetness doesn't make me a snob. It just means that I know the proper way to drink iced tea." Marc took a sip of his unsweet tea and sighed. "So good. I don't even know how you can taste the actual tea in that sweet stuff."

"Who knew my boyfriend was so *proper*," I joked and then froze. We hadn't exactly labeled what we had. If we were going to try the whole long-distance thing, would boyfriends be the right descriptor?

"Your boyfriend can be as proper as they come, but I think I'd like to get very improper with my *boyfriend* in his truck." Marc's eyes gleamed as we stared at each other across the cab of the truck.

So, yeah, I guess boyfriends was what we were.

Holy shit.

Who knew that a stop in that Shilesville bar would lead me to falling in love and having a boyfriend?

"Well, your boyfriend is very interested in assisting you in all of your impropriety." I hurried from the truck and hauled the basket from the back.

We worked quickly to bag up our trash, pack up any leftovers, and return everything to the basket which I then tossed back into the truck bed.

Once I was back in the truck, I moved close to Marc and wrapped him in a tight embrace before devouring his mouth. He tasted of tea, strawberries, and lust, but also of promise, longing, and devotion. No other man had ever sown himself so deeply into my life, my heart. Hell, all the way into my soul.

We ended up stripped to various degrees of nakedness. Which meant I lost my shirt, and my jeans and underwear were bunched around my ankles. Marc's boots made their way over to the driver side floorboard, his clothes laid in a pile in the driver's seat—hopefully my shirt was in the bundle—and he straddled my lap wearing only his socks.

Our cocks rubbed together, his balls pressed against the base of my shaft, as he rocked his hips and arched his back. I teased his nipples with my tongue before biting gently and soothing with my lips. Pressing kisses along his collarbone to his neck to his jawline, I pulled Marc into a searing kiss.

He whimpered as our tongues met and I ran my hands

down his back to grip his ass. Trailing a finger between his cheeks, I tapped lightly against his hole.

"Wanna ride you," he whispered breathily against my ear. "Please, Jordan. Give me that cock, stretch me open."

I groaned as my dick dribbled precum onto my stomach, or maybe it was Marc's, or a mixture of both. "Glove compartment," I bit out. "Under the registration; there's lube."

Marc chuckled. "Always prepared." He rifled through the glove box and proudly produced the bottle.

"Nah, threw it in there this morning. Just in case. Didn't want a repeat of our first time at the river or being reduced to using just spit." I took the lube and slicked a finger, moving to his ass and smearing his entrance before slipping one, then two, fingers into him.

Marc took the bottle from me. "Can you shift down a bit, so your hips hang a bit off the seat?"

It wasn't the most comfortable position, and I prayed no one else would come to this exact spot—tinted windows or not, they'd totally be able to see Marc's naked body riding me.

He dribbled lube on my dick and coated me with a few pumps of his fist. Then he moved so he was straddling my waist a bit more, reached behind, and gripped my shaft. I watched his face and savored the sensation of his hand on me, my head pressing against his hot opening. My body hummed as sensation took over. I adored the look of ecstasy on Marc's face as his body opened to accept my cock. His tight heat, taking me in inch-by-glorious-inch, was enough to make my breath hitch. I gripped his hips and waited until he bottomed out. With his balls pressed against me, his throbbing shaft bobbing between us, and his head thrown back, Marc embodied the definition of beauty. So gorgeous, so passionate, so *mine*. It was no wonder I'd fallen so head-over-heels in love with him.

"Fuck, that's so good," he panted, rocking his hips. "Love the way you fill me."

I gave short, sharp thrusts of my hips as my hands caressed his back. When I ran my nails up and down his spine, he arched his back. "Mmmm, you look so good like this. Your back arched; so pretty. Your cock begging for release. Your hot little hole taking me so deep."

Marc whimpered and increased the speed of his rocking, encouraging me to thrust harder and faster. "Touch me," he begged. "Wanna come."

I took his cock in my hand and began to stroke, thumbing his slit and smearing the bead of precum. I shifted my position, sitting up so we were chest-to-chest. The angle was awkward, but I continued to jack him between our bodies as I captured his lips and kissed him in the same rhythm as my fist on his shaft and my cock in his ass.

I knew he was close by the sexy little noises he made. Within seconds, Marc tore his mouth from mine, threw his head back, and groaned as his cock spilled his release over my fingers. He pulsed in my hand as he panted. "Move back down and fuck me; wanna feel your cum in me."

Knowing it wouldn't take more than a few pumps of my hips before I blew, I shifted back down in the seat, my legs supporting me and allowing for harder thrusting. I watched Marc's blissed-out face as I gripped his hips and began to thrust hard and fast. His tight little hole greedily taking me deep, his chest flushed, his hands smearing his cum on my stomach. When he brought a cum-wet finger to my mouth, I groaned as I licked the digit clean, my balls drawing up tight as a tingle traveled through me.

With one final thrust, my cock exploded in hot, sticky spurts as I filled Marc's ass with my release. I sat up again, plastering our chests together and kissed him as I continued to unload deep inside of him. Selfishly—almost caveman-ish —I loved that he'd never taken another man bare. I loved knowing that no other man's cum had ever filled him and leaked from his hole.

"Fuck," Marc panted. "So good." He shifted a knee and winced. "So awkward and uncomfortable," he joked, "but so damn hot." He leaned in to kiss me, our lips and tongues slower and more sensual than the frenzy of earlier. "I love you so much."

My cock gave one last twitch and I groaned when Marc clenched his ass around me. "I love you," I whispered against his lips.

We eventually separated, cleaned ourselves, redressed, and headed home. Another experience at *our* river for the memory books.

ELEVEN

MARC

"ARE YOU FREAKIN' kidding me?" I slammed my hand on the steering wheel as I fumed. Gran had asked me to run into town to drop a few things at the post office and get some groceries. She had guests at the BnB and preferred to stay on-site if possible. Gran was an amazing host, always so welcoming. Most guests seemed to consider her an old friend pretty much from the moment they arrived.

"What's wrong?" Jordan's voice asked from the car's speakers.

"Why are there about fifty damn tractors on the road? On the actual road!"

There was a pause and then Jordan's laughter rang out. "It must be Farm and Field Day at the school."

"That doesn't answer why there are fifty tractors traveling down the road and blocking my way!"

"It's a day when all the kids drive their tractors to school. There are probably more like seventy-five if we're getting technical." I heard the chickens in the background and knew Jordan was in the coop.

"Tell my girls hi and I'll be home..." I paused. "Well, I

was going to say *soon* but it may take *days* at this rate. Who the hell thought this was a good idea?"

Jordan was quiet for a moment and I wondered if I'd lost him, but then his voice came through again. "It's a long-standing tradition. Remember when I mentioned it and you said, and I quote, *No tractor is going to irk me*." He laughed.

"Yeah, well, I thought you meant *a* tractor. Not a herd of tractors!" I gripped the steering wheel and fought the urge to scream. "This is insane!"

"Not sure *herd* is accurate," he said with a chuckle. The sound of happy hens floated through the speaker; he'd likely just given them some grapes and tomatoes—which I'd been shocked to learn they were not only allowed to eat, but they *loved* the treat. "You've got time. Ellie doesn't need the groceries *right now* and you'll get to the post office once all the kids pass. You should pull over at the next field entrance and watch them go by. You'll see a wide variety I'm sure."

"There's a wide variety of *tractors*? I figured a tractor was a tractor." I drew in a deep breath and blew it out slowly.

"Oh, Oxford, you still have so much to learn," Jordan teased.

My heart caught. I had just over a week left before I returned to Rockhurst. In all honesty, I wasn't dealing well with it. As in, I wasn't dealing with it at all. I'd shoved reality aside and chosen instead to focus on Jordan and the BnB and pretend my world wasn't going to come to a screeching halt in a matter of days.

"Hey, I need to get these veggies to the roadside stand. Take time to watch the tractors," Jordan said.

"Is that similar to *Take time to smell the roses*?" I scoffed.

"Yep, it's the Kingsley version. Take a breath, enjoy the sunshine, and watch the tractors. I bet you'll be surprised at what you see."

We said goodbye and I took the next little field entrance,

glad that it was empty—Jordan had explained the field was fallow which was kinda like giving it a break from growing things for a season. I would have *never* driven *my* car into a dusty field, but Gran insisted her car was made for country living. I maneuvered the vehicle so I was off the road and facing the four-way stop where tractors were coming from three directions.

After rolling down the windows and taking a few deep breaths of the country air, I decided—much to my chagrin, but it was beginning to be my norm—that Jordan was right. The tractors were a very impressive sight.

It seemed that it didn't matter the type or age or size of the tractor, the kids were just happy to drive it to school—and they were definitely *kids*; I swore most of the drivers were around thirteen to seventeen. *Things are different in Kingsley.* I began to categorize—based on my very limited knowledge of the machines—into four categories.

First, there were the small tractors that reminded me a lot of Jordan's lawn mower. I'd been shocked the first time he said he was going to mow the BnB yard along with his own and he pulled out a mammoth vehicle that truly looked like a mini tractor—or at least similar. The kids driving these had the advantage in speed and maneuverability—I liked the fact that *they* wouldn't have taken up the entire damn road.

Second, and while still interesting to see, were the plain ol' run-of-the-mill tractors. They weren't flashy or huge, didn't have the antique feel. I was still impressed by them and the fact young kids were driving them, but they didn't stand out. They were kind of just the standard image of a tractor you might see on a news story—maybe like the stock image of tractors.

Third, there were the old tractors. Like *really old*. I was surprised that most of them still started let alone held it together long enough to make a trip to and from school.

Maybe there was truth to the whole *don't make 'em like they used to* phrase. The machines chugged and sputtered as they moved slowly along, but they were aesthetically pleasing in a nostalgic type way—made me wonder what it would have been like in Kingsley back when those tractors were the newest and best models.

Fourth, these things had my eyes bugging out of my head, were the largest and flashiest—definitely most expensive—machines. These were few and far between; I think I saw only three in the whole parade. But *damn*, they were impressive. Two passed right in front of me and I wasn't exaggerating to say they took up the entire road plus some. The third came from the other road leading to the four-way-stop and as I watched it crawl along a sudden thought slammed into me. How in the hell was that monster going to make the turn at the stop sign? The beast in no way had that type of turning radius. I glanced nervously to the intersection and realized someone had already thought ahead. Two of the four stop signs were missing.

I waited with baited breath to see if the behemoth would be able to make the turn. Several of the drivers had stopped completely and hung out their windows, leaned over their steering wheels, or stood from their smaller vehicles to watch the spectacle.

The driver of the large tractor coming up to the right turn appeared to be older than most of the younger kids I'd seen. In fact, I'd guess he was a grown man. Maybe a teacher at the school? He gave a wave before taking hold of the wheel with both hands and executing the most perfect turn I could have imagined for the large farm equipment.

Hoots and hollers erupted from the other drivers and the parade continued. When the last tractor—possibly the oldest one I'd seen, or at least the most run-down—finally puttered through the intersection, a large pickup truck similar to

Jordan's followed. The driver stopped at the stop sign, left his truck, returned the removed signs to their rightful positions, climbed back into his truck, and drove off.

I sat for several moments processing what I'd just seen. While it *had* been an annoyance—it was good I didn't have anywhere urgent I needed to be—I was glad I'd stopped to watch instead of stewing and fuming while stuck in the line. I still wasn't sure what the purpose of the event was exactly, but it had seemed like something that the participants enjoyed.

As I pulled back onto the road, I decided to follow the tractors. Perhaps a glutton for punishment? But I wanted to watch the long line pull into the junior high and high school parking lot. I knew the school was small—likely no more than one hundred and twenty-five in the whole building from seventh to twelfth grade—so I assumed well over half of the students had driven their tractors to school that day.

As I neared the school, I realized the Farm and Field Day was something the entire town looked forward to. There were several people lined up to watch the parade of machines crawl by. Little kids—some not even old enough to head on over to the elementary school when the parade was complete—sat perched on their parents' shoulders and cheered.

I smiled as I pulled into an open parking spot—the only one available due to the crowd—and climbed from the car to watch the line of tractors make their way into the long driveway that led to the older school building. Jordan had explained that both schools had been built when he was little—up until then, all grades were housed in one location—but they'd been kept in pristine condition and updated regularly. He and Gran had both boasted that Kingsley was actually a force to be reckoned with in academics as well as basketball. And the football team was supposedly pretty decent, too.

Grabbing the packages from the backseat, I headed

toward the post office three blocks down. After a quick stop at the grocery I'd head on home. I couldn't help but chuckle and shake my head. Only in Kingsley could I get stuck in a tractor parade. That shit wouldn't fly in Rockhurst. Three months ago, I would have thought that shit wouldn't fly with me. But, thanks to Jordan, thanks to Gran, thanks to the sunshine and fresh air, I found myself strangely connected to the tractor parade. And the townsfolk just gathering on the sidewalks to visit. And the nosey postal worker. And the tiny grocery store with the creaky door, squeaky floors, but pretty much every staple you could possibly need.

In Rockhurst, I could walk two blocks to find a thirty-two theater mega-movie-complex. In Kingsley, we needed to drive an hour for a big theater—or to Shilesville where they had one tiny theater that showed movies that were at least a year old. But I'd take a movie projected on a sheet on the side of the shed and cuddling in the back of Jordan's truck any damn day.

In Rockhurst, I could order from Amazon and have it delivered that day—at the most, the next day. In Kingsley, the two-day delivery wasn't ever guaranteed. And when it did show up, you likely had to drive to town and spend a minimum of twenty minutes chatting with LeeAnn at the post office.

In Rockhurst, I had my choice of twenty different restaurants within a four-block radius that would deliver in under thirty minutes. In Kingsley, I had Gran's kitchen table or a fish place Jordan didn't trust, a Chinese place that was surprisingly good, pizza, and Candle Light Diner. Aside from missing sushi, I'd take Gran's cooking and the limited choices of Kingsley every damn time. Hell, I'd take frozen pizza and domestic beer on the couch with Jordan.

As I walked toward my car with my arms full of brown paper grocery bags—which I knew Jordan reused or repurposed into the compost pile for his gardens, my throat tightened as my brain and heart tried to wrap around the fact that I'd not only fallen in love with Jordan, but also with Kingsley. And I was leaving in a matter of days.

But what were my other options? My *job* was in Rockhurst. My apartment—sparse and lonely as it was. I wasn't even going to use *friends* as an excuse anymore—no one in the city could bring me as much joy as Jordan. Hell, I'd take Gran over any of my so-called friends. I *was* excited to see my sister again. And Gramps. But other than those two, I really had nothing calling me back to the city but a job.

A job you love I reminded myself.

I sighed. Leaving a man I loved, and a place I loved, to return to a job I loved wasn't as cut-and-dry and simple as the prospect had seemed three months ago. Hell, three months ago the thought of loving this place and this man would have never even entered my mind.

I called Jordan on my way back home.

"How are the tractors?" Jordan asked with a smile in his voice as he picked up.

"Parade is done. I'm heading home." It wasn't lost on me that I'd begun to refer to the BnB and Jordan's farm as *home*.

"Did you enjoy it?"

"Actually, yes. I didn't realize there were so many different types. Three of them were monsters."

"Yeah, I thought you'd be impressed by those. The amount of money you watched travel past would blow your mind," Jordan said.

"Like how much are we talking?" I'd known the machines were costly, but I wasn't sure *how* costly.

"Well, the ones like mine probably cost about five grand. The standards run anywhere between twenty and thirty grand. The old ones will definitely range; they probably didn't cost much back then, but they were expensive for the times.

But now—especially if they're in good shape—they're considered antiques so they'd fetch quite a bit at auction." Noises came through the speakers that sounded like wood being stacked so I assumed he was in the workshop. "Those three big boys—and keep in mind that those aren't even the top of top of the line—probably ran fifty to seventy-five thousand."

I whistled. "Damn. And there are even bigger ones?"

"Yeah, some of the biggest, newest, most technologically advanced will set a person back about one hundred and twenty grand. All run by computer systems. They're impressive, but kinda crazy to me."

"People in Kingsley have the money for a seventy-five-thousand-dollar tractor?" I asked.

"Not many, but yeah, a few farms have that type money."

"How?"

"Well, the majority of the farmers in Kingsley have smaller amounts of land, sell to the local grain elevator or work with a couple nearby towns." A scratchy sound I'd come to associate with sandpaper filled the air as Jordan sanded whatever project he was working on. "But three of the farms are original landowners from way back when. Well, the descendants of the originals."

"Like a monopoly where they own all the land?" That didn't seem quite fair.

"Way back when, yeah, it was kinda like that. But in the past twenty to thirty years, those three farms have hatched deals with large corporations. So, their crops don't add or subtract from Kingsley's economy; all of their harvests go straight to corporate contracts and are divvied out from there. It's actually a good thing for the town because when the trucks come in for the haul—or even when the corporate suits come for meetings—the town gets a bit of an uptick. Those farms provide about twenty of the townsfolk with jobs. They had to add a line and a stop for a specific train to be able to come through during harvest and pick up grain. So that was about seven new jobs as well."

I processed the information. "Well, it sounds like it's an agreeable situation for all involved." I paused. "Wait. Does that mean there will be *more* train noise in the fall?"

Jordan chuckled. "Hardly even notice it. But you'll be in Rockhurst, so your precious ears will be saved, Oxford."

I had a feeling Jordan continually reminded me of my departure as a way of keeping his own feelings in check, but damn, it sucked to always have that reminder. "Yeah, but I'll visit. Note to self: avoid the fall."

"Nah, fall is an amazing time in Kingsley. The trees paint the town with an explosion of colorful leaves. The air is crisp with just the right amount of bite. Campfires, pumpkin spice bread, cinnamon, flannel."

I chuckled. "I take it you're a fan?"

"I love fall, definitely."

"Guess I'll suffer through the train then." I pulled into Gran's driveway. "Hey, gonna deliver these groceries and visit with Gran. I'll be over later."

"Wanna build the bird houses?"

"Perfect."

I carried the bags of groceries toward the BnB. Based on the cars in the drive, I was guessing a few guests had left for some sight-seeing. I saw one couple heading out toward the little pond. And two women were sitting on the back patio with what appeared to be bread and strawberry jam to complement their tea.

"There's my boy. Did you have any trouble?" Gran came and patted my cheek. She tried to take one of the bags, but I insisted on carrying the whole load to the kitchen.

"Trouble? Like a nosy postal worker? The grocery being out of the *good* flour? Or a parade of tractors five miles long?"

Gran's eyes went wide. "Oh, my goodness. Today must be Farm and Field Day at school. I can't believe I forgot."

I shrugged. "It's okay. At first, I was pissed off, but I ended up enjoying it."

"I wasn't apologizing to you, Marcus." Gran's sharp eyes held humor. "I'm glad you got to experience it. I just feel bad that I didn't tell the guests."

I rolled my eyes and attempted to let her lack of compassion for my suffering roll off my back. "Well, there's always the return trip. Maybe have them go into town and watch as they leave school?"

"That's perfect." She smiled. "Maybe we'll take a couple cars and make it a big group thing."

I tensed, hoping she wasn't going to ask for my help. I'd enjoyed the tractors and I'd help Gran in any way I could. But I was really looking forward to spending one of my last days with Jordan.

"Calm yourself, child. I don't need you moping around here and bringing my guests down. You're welcome to spend as much of your remaining time with Jordan as you'd like." Her eyes dimmed. "I hate to think of how miserable and broken you'll both be when you leave. I can't say I think what you boys have is a mistake, but I'm wondering just how smart it was to get involved when you knew the ending." Then she tsked. "But, I did want you two to be friends; I was right that you're good for each other. I'm just concerned about the upcoming heartbreak."

"We're going to make it work. We can totally do the long-distance thing. It's not like we're across the world from each other. Two hours is nothing. I'll be here so much you'll likely be sick of me." I figured the more times I said it, the more likely it was to sink in. So far, my words held a lot more confidence than I actually felt.

"I'll never grow sick of you, Marcus." She took my hand.

"I want more than anything for you and Jordan to be happy. Gramps and I make it work; true, it's a slightly different situation, but I can see it working for you boys."

"Jordan's biggest concern is that it's not just a temporary fix. We're stuck with our locations. He can't leave the farm—and, of course, I'd never expect him to. And I can't leave the city. So, we're facing an entire relationship of constant long-distance and only seeing each other on visits." I shared Jordan's worries, but I'd decided to be our cheering section—convinced we could make it work; we loved each other after all—rather than being down and negative about the situation.

"I understand his worries; they're very valid. I also think you two have found something special with each other; the love crackles between you like a magic spell. Even when you were trying to hide it, there was no doubt—at least in my mind." Gran smiled softly. "But I'm not one hundred percent sure you're *stuck* in your locations. Maybe stuck in your mind. Stuck in your ways. Stuck in what you *think* is right." She gave my hand a squeeze. "Now, I've got guests to visit with, bread to bake, and lunch to fix. You give that man of yours a hug and kiss for me. I'll see you sometime tomorrow."

I kissed her cheek and gave her a hug. "Love you."

As I headed towards Jordan's I couldn't stop Gran's words bouncing and crashing around in my head. Was I truly not stuck? Did I have other options? Did I *want* other options? Could I stay?

I found Jordan in the workshop where he'd finished another rocking chair and added more to the bed he'd been working on. As expected, pretty much every piece we'd advertised at the BnB and on the website had brought in orders. The most lucrative so far had been a table and chair set; it was absolutely gorgeous and I wanted one for myself.

But of course, it wouldn't match my sleek and nearly bare apartment.

I wrapped my arms around Jordan's waist and kissed the back of his neck. "Hi. Gran said to give you a hug and kiss for her."

His shoulders shook slightly as he chuckled and turned in my arms. "Oh, she did, did she?" He pulled me close and captured my lips in a soul-searing kiss. "Pretty sure this wasn't what she had in mind."

"I sure as hell hope not," I teased before diving back in to worship his mouth.

"Let's get these built. Then we can use our time for *other* activities after chores and a shower." Jordan gave me one final tender kiss and brushed his thumb over my lips as if sealing the kiss.

We worked to build a set of six birdhouses. Two were going to Gran, three were to fulfill an order, and I was taking one back to Rockhurst. I watched Jordan make the first one. Assisted with the next four—him having me do a bit more on my own with each tiny house. And then I made the sixth one completely on my own.

Three months ago, I never would have *wanted* to make a birdhouse let alone thought I'd be able to. But now, I felt a strange sense of pride and accomplishment as I looked at my own creation and the ones I'd helped with.

"These will look great on Gran's fence row." I turned my own little house over in my hands. "Not sure exactly what good this will do me in the city, but I love it. Maybe it will just be decoration in my room."

Jordan's eyes clouded for a moment. "A little piece of Kingsley to take back with you."

I walked into his arms and shuddered as he held me tight. "Pretty sure I'm taking a lot more than a birdhouse back with me."

"A birdhouse and my entire heart." His words were choked with emotion against my ear and I buried my head against his neck.

AFTER CHORES AND SEPARATE SHOWERS, we ate a light dinner before Jordan told me he had a surprise for me in the workshop.

"Let me get it ready," he said. "I'll text you when you can come out."

Wondering what in the world he could have out there that I hadn't already seen earlier in the day, I settled on the couch with my phone to wait on his message. He'd walked out of the house in just his lounge pants and a t-shirt, so I assumed I'd be presentable in just my lounge pants. Just as I was wondering if I should go put on a t-shirt, my phone buzzed.

Jordan: *Come on out and tell me if you like what you see.*

I twisted my lips at the coy little message. Jordan flirting was both adorable and hot. I scrambled from the couch, telling my dick not to get too excited because it was probably just a carving or similar, and headed toward the workshop.

My phone buzzed again.

Jordan: *Lock the door behind you when you get here.*

I was beyond intrigued.

The workshop windows had curtains, but no blinds, and I saw a dim light coming from the side facing the house. Jordan had the floor lamps he used for *ambience* turned on, but not the bright, overhead, fluorescent lights he used when he was working on a project.

Pushing the side door open, I closed it quietly behind me and locked it. The floor felt cool on my bare feet—and who the hell had I become? Walking around *barefoot*? This place had truly changed me. But I knew the floor of Jordan's workshop was meticulously swept every day and clean enough to eat from.

As my eyes adjusted to the dim lighting, the act of breathing suddenly became a challenge. There before me, leaning against his homemade, waist-high workbench that filled the entire back wall of the shop, Jordan stood with his legs spread, flannel-clad arms crossed over a bare chest under an unbuttoned camo-patterned shirt, and nothing else but a pair of unlaced work boots.

My dick instantly went from mildly curious to *hell yes, right here, right now*. I groaned as I palmed my erection and moved closer. How in the fucking hell was a nearly naked man in undone work boots so damn sexy? "What the hell is this? Are you *trying* to kill me?" The heat and lust were thick between us, making my words gravely and low.

Fire and mischief danced in Jordan's eyes and he shrugged slightly as his rock-hard cock stood tall, proudly bobbing in the most tantalizing of invitations. "Just thought I'd see if I could give you a reason to like camo and a memory to take to the city." He winked and licked his lips. "Two birds, one stone."

"Who knew my farm boy was such a sexy tease?" I stood close enough that I knew the moment I removed my pants, our cocks would meet, their leaking slits kissing. Heat flashed between us and my desire flared, want and need flooding my veins. The workshop air was slightly cool and my nipples hardened as I took in the gorgeous sight before me. "Never gonna love camo, but if *this*," I gestured toward him, "is the prize, a bitch sure will make an exception."

Jordan's perfect lips twisted into a sensual smile. "Hoped you say that." He reached for the waistband of my pants and pulled the elastic down under my balls. "Love that you don't put on underwear at night." He took hold of my throbbing dick and I stepped closer as if compelled by a magnetic attraction. I tossed my phone onto the workbench behind him and let my hands rest on his chest. My thumbs teased his nipples as his large hand engulfed our cocks and began to stroke.

"What's your plan here?" I asked breathlessly, my forehead resting against his as I watched our hard, leaking cocks slide in and out of his fist.

"Up to you where we start, but my endgame is to bury myself in your ass and fill you as you scream my name," Jordan growled and continued to pump our shafts.

"Fuuuuck," I groaned. "Yeah, I can get on board with that." I tipped his chin and devoured his mouth, my tongue stroking and teasing. I broke the kiss and pressed my lips along his jawline as my hands pushed the camouflage flannel from his shoulders. I kissed and licked his neck and shoulders before grabbing one of the workshop towels he kept folded on a shelf. Keeping it folded for better cushion, I placed it on the ground, stripped my pants off, and dropped to my knees.

I gripped Jordan's hips and buried my face against his groin, savoring the heat and scent of him. I spread my knees wider to find a comfortable position, and found myself in sensation overload when the roughness of his work boots abraded the bare skin of my legs. Jordan shifted to let the shirt drop from his body and I was faced with a completely naked man wearing only work boots—which were right at that moment roughly reminding me of their presence with each slight movement of my legs.

With my eyes trained on Jordan's, the bite of his boots against my legs, and my cock already begging for release, I fisted his dick and swirled my tongue around his head. "Wanna taste you, but don't come yet," I ordered before sucking him deep and savoring the sexy sounds he made as he rocked his hips and took my mouth.

Part of me—the part that adored sucking Jordan off—wanted him to give me his release, let me swallow him and lick him clean. But the other part of me—the greedy bottom begging for that cock to be buried in my ass when he came apart—wanted more. I sucked him and fondled his balls for a moment longer, before popping off and standing to kiss him as our dicks pressed together. "Ready for that endgame plan?"

Jordan moaned into my mouth and walked me toward a drawer unit against the other wall. The top didn't completely reach my waist and put me at a perfect height when I bent at the waist, my chest flush against the cool wood, my hard nipples thrilling at the bite of the rough texture.

I spread my legs and glanced over my shoulder. "Any time now, country boy." I wiggled my ass, my heavy balls swinging as I fought the urge to thrust against the drawers.

Jordan reached for a bottle of lube I hadn't even noticed—I loved the fact he'd planned our encounter so thoroughly—but instead of slicking his cock and sliding in, he put the bottle aside and plastered his chest to my back, nipping at my ear and groaning as I whimpered. "I love you. I think I've loved you a little bit since the night at the river. And even more when you showed up in your spiffy Oxfords to pick veggies. I dread you leaving, but I will do whatever it takes to make this work because being apart from you will be enough of a nightmare. I don't want to try to imagine what it would be like to lose you completely."

I turned my head and opened for his plundering tongue as he kissed me. When we broke, both panting, I smiled. "I love you, too. Maybe since the river. Maybe since you first called me Oxford. But no matter when this love *started*, I know I never want it to end."

He made quick work of smearing lube on his cock and slicking my hole. When I knew he would prefer to prep me, I thrust my hips back. "Just fuck me, don't want prep. Need you in me."

Jordan would have normally ignored my request and worked me open at least a bit, but this time he complied, lining his head up with my entrance and slowly pushing inside.

I bit back a gasp at the sudden bite of pain, but I breathed through it as Jordan gave my body time to adjust. "More," I begged.

He pushed deeper, giving me more of his impressive length, until I tensed and clenched around him.

Loving that he knew how to work my body so well, I waited just a moment as the stinging stretch gave way to a warm fullness—ridiculously full, but oh so good. I reached behind me to grip his hips and pulled him forward, taking the rest of his cock balls deep. "God, so good. So full."

"You're so damn tight," Jordan bit out. "Wanna move." He hissed when I clenched my hole around his wide girth.

"Move. I'm ready, want it all," I begged.

Jordan's hands took hold of my hips, his fingers protecting my hip bones from the rough edge of the countertop. He began to thrust, long and slow at first, picking up speed until the slap of skin, the slick slide of his cock, and our heavy breathing were the only sounds that filled the room.

Too soon, his frantic thrusts slowed and he pressed his chest against my back. "Gonna fuck you long and slow until you shoot your load down the front of this cabinet," he whispered in my ear.

"Want you to come, too," I panted.

"Oh, I will. I'll follow right behind and fill your pretty city boy ass with my cum," he promised.

My balls drew up tight and I reached to stroke my cock.

Jordan kept an agonizingly slow pace, his cock glancing

against my prostate, until I couldn't hold back. I increased my speed and grip and jacked myself until my release roared through me and I painted the drawers.

As my orgasm continued to rock me, Jordan's thrusts became harder and harder until he tensed and let loose in my ass on a long groan. His liquid heat filled me and I clenched tightly around his shaft, milking him for every drop.

We lay slumped over the drawer unit for several moments as we caught our breath. Then, after a long, sweet kiss, we gathered the few clothes we'd brought with us, turned off the lights, and returned to the house.

Without words, Jordan toed off his boots and took my hand as he followed me up the stairs. We climbed into bed and wrapped up in each other's arms. After a long, leisurely kiss, we dozed with the mutual knowledge that we'd be worshipping each other's bodies again before morning.

TWELVE
JORDAN

MARC GROANED and lifted his leg as he rolled halfway to his stomach. "Give it to me," he begged.

We'd slept for a few hours, but my cock was awake and very interested in returning to its favorite place. I pushed a finger into Marc's ass and growled when I felt the leftover lube and cum from earlier. Smearing a bit of it around his pucker, I took hold of my shaft and slid deep inside of him with one long thrust.

Marc cried out, his finger nails biting into the arm I had wrapped around his chest.

"Too much?" I asked against his ear.

"No, so good. Hard and fast," he demanded.

I rocked my hips, thrusting hard, my cock pumping deep into his tight hole.

"Stroke me," Marc begged.

His dick throbbed in my fist as I thumbed his slit and pumped his shaft. I knew from his breathy whimpers and panting moans that he was about to blow. I continued to stroke him in the same rhythm as my cock in his ass.

When his head dropped back onto my shoulder and his

release spilled over my fingers, I increased my speed until my balls tightened and I pulsed my hot seed deep into his ass.

Moments later, after catching our breaths, we wiped ourselves clean. No words were shared, only kisses and sensual touches, before we wrapped ourselves in each other's arms and settled in for a few more hours of sleep.

Just when I thought Marc was asleep and I'd soon be joining him, his words broke through the sated silence of the room.

"What if I stayed?" he blurted, his voice nowhere near as sleepy as I would have expected.

"What?" I yelped.

He propped up on an elbow. "What if I stayed? What if I just didn't go back?"

My heart soared. Marc staying was my one and only dream. And he was insinuating that he could make that dream come true. *Yes. Stay. It's the only thing I've ever wanted. You're the only thing I've ever wanted.* I thought of Marc's words the day of the tractor parade. *Tell the girls I'll be home soon.* Could Marc really ever consider Kingsley home? Could he find his home with a country boy chicken and vegetable farmer? Watching him with the chickens, helping with the BnB, and being part of my everyday life, I wanted so badly to think *yes, yes, he could.*

But despite how high my heart flew, it almost instantly crashed to the hard ground. No. No, I couldn't let Marc sacrifice his own life, his own dreams, just to make mine come true.

I caressed the side of his face. "While every cell of my being wants to beg you to do just that, you can't."

"The fuck I can't," he growled.

I shook my head. "No, I won't let you do it. Eventually, you'd regret it. You'd always wonder *what if*. You'd miss your job." My heart pinched. "You'd end up blaming me. The heartbreak of you leaving will be bad enough. I couldn't stand to have you resent me because you didn't go back and live your life in the city."

Marc shook his head. "What if my life is no longer in the city? What if my life started the day I met you?"

I refused to hope that he spoke the truth. "Then that's something you have to figure out on your own. You have to go live that city life again and find out it's no longer where your heart is. I can't allow you to stay without knowing you've exhausted the other options."

His features fell. "You're right. I have to let this thing play out the way it was meant to. At least tell me you'd want me to stay if I could."

"More than my next breath," I whispered.

He curled against my chest and my tears fell silently into his hair before I could stop them.

THE DAY MARC was scheduled to leave dawned as damp and dreary as I felt. We spent our last wake-up wrapped together, savoring the most intimate of moments, memorizing each other's bodies as if our lives depended on it.

Maybe it was dramatic, but I kinda couldn't help but think my life *did* depend on the memories of Marc. I'd known the day would come. I'd known I'd be broken. I was beyond grateful that today wasn't an official, *forever* goodbye. But the everyday, close connection we'd had for three months was something I'd come to thrive on. When Marc drove away, I'd have only the memories to get me through.

"You're thinking too much," Marc whispered as he held me tight. "We'll talk every day. If you're not visiting me, I'll be here. My thought is that I'll come visit at least every other weekend." He kissed the side of my head.

I nodded, but said nothing because I didn't trust my voice.

We eventually climbed from bed—we'd pushed chores until the very latest moment allowable—just as a train rumbled by.

Marc paused in pulling on his work jeans. "Is it weird that I no longer even notice Hank's obnoxious noises and the train almost feels soothing?"

I pressed the back of my hand to his forehead and pretended to be concerned. "Are you feeling okay? Fever? Chills? Weakness?"

Marc laughed and batted away my hand. "It's just crazy how much I've changed in three months. Gramps always said this place grows on you; I definitely know what he means now."

I cocked my head and studied him. "I don't know. I'm not sure this place has *changed* you."

He frowned. "What do you mean? You can't possibly think I'm the same as the first day you met me."

"No. But it's not so much about Kingsley changing you. I think it's more about this place—and I'd like to think maybe the company you've been keeping—allowing you to let your guard down. You've been allowed to relax—something I'm not sure you've ever really been allowed to do. Maybe you haven't changed so much as the *real* you, the person you've always been, the person you truly *want* to be, has had a chance to spread his wings and be seen." I shrugged. "Maybe that sounds ridiculous."

Marc cupped my face and kissed me. "No, it doesn't. It sounds accurate. I'm not a different person after being here. I'm the same person, but the real me has had a chance to come out." He kissed me again. "And he's never going back to hiding. I like the more relaxed, easy-going version of me."

I smiled and hugged him tight. I pushed away the worry that within one day back in the city, the *real* Marc would immediately be drowned out by the stress and tension of his job, his father, his day-to-day life. "Come on, the girls need their breakfast and we need their eggs."

After finishing with the chickens—I swore Marc wanted to gather them all in a hug—we picked the veggies, grateful for the lack of sunshine to keep the job cooler since we'd waited so late.

Our last stop for the morning was at the strawberry plants.

The plants were chock-full of green berries.

"Damn it, I so wanted at least one ripe one before I left," Marc grumbled as he lifted leaves looking for a prize I knew he wasn't going to find. "I don't want to leave without seeing them to the end."

I wrapped my arms around his waist as he straightened to his full height. "So, the strawberry plants are the only thing you don't want to leave?"

He turned in my arms and hugged me tight. "The list of things I don't want to leave has grown exponentially and you're at the top."

"I think maybe we should let you get settled in before we decide who is visiting and when," I suggested. "Once you're back into your schedule, we can better make plans."

"I don't like it," Marc stated, "but it makes sense. Give me the rest of this week and the weekend to get acclimated and back into a routine. Then we can figure out if you're coming to see me or if I'm coming here."

"Just remember that I can't leave at the drop of a hat. I also can't be gone constantly." I loved my life, my farm, my business, but part of me held regret toward those things for keeping me tied down and away from Marc. But even without my responsibilities in Kingsley, could I ever be truly happy in the city?

"Keep in mind, you have help now. Maybe not enough help to leave for weeks at a time, but Ms. Bethany and Scott can handle the day-to-day. And you know Gran will help as well. She's pretty much said she'll run your whole damn farm herself it if means we get some time together."

"I know. I completely trust them all..."

"But?" Marc pushed.

"But I feel guilty. Ellie isn't a spring chicken and it's not fair to put so much physical labor on her. Ms. Bethany and Scott are a lot younger, but it's still not fair to turn their part-time jobs into full-time."

"First, they've both indicated they'd be happy with extra hours. Second, I'm not going to tell Gran you called her old, but she'd kick your ass if she knew you were using that as an excuse."

We puttered around with final bits and pieces of chores and went to Ellie's for lunch.

All too soon, Marc headed upstairs to gather his belongings.

"You boys are going to be just fine," Ellis promised as she patted my hand.

I tried to smile, but a heavy weight had settled in my gut.

Marc kept on a happy face as he hugged his grandmother and said goodbye with a promise to return soon.

Then the two of us were alone in the driveway.

Marc tossed his bag in his car. "This isn't goodbye. We're going to make this work." He lifted my chin. "We're still on the same page with that, right? You want to make this work?"

I blinked away tears and nodded. "More than anything.

Just going to take a bit to get used to you being gone. My bed is going to feel empty without you."

He kissed me. "I love you."

I leaned into him, savoring the love and promise of the kiss. "I love you," I whispered. "Be safe. Text me when you're back at your place?"

Marc nodded, pressed one last kiss to my lips, and climbed into his car.

And then I watched my heart drive away.

"DID you know he tried to stay?" I asked a week later over coffee and pie with Ellie. We'd gotten out of the breakfast habit while Marc was in Kingsley, but she'd been my rock since he left.

She glanced at me over her coffee mug. "Interesting. What did you say to that?"

I shrugged. "That I wanted more than anything for him to stay, but that he'd regret it—resent me—if he didn't go back."

Ellie was quiet for a moment. "I think you're right. But I also think Marcus was right. Staying—or coming back as the case may be—is a viable option for him. He's just going to have to figure that out for himself. It needs to be his decision and not something he does because he thinks it's what you or I want him to do."

"We've been talking every day. He's back to having headaches, stomach issues, and night sweats." I frowned. "I'm not sure if he's telling me exactly how bad it is. But his voice sounds off and the few times we've done video chat, he's looked like shit."

Ellie's brow furrowed. "What's he say about work?" She took a bite of pie.

"That it's taking him a lot longer to get back into the routine. He's had a few go-rounds with his dad. The only time he sounds happy is when he talks about Gramps or Marissa."

"Ed says Marcus seems off, definitely not himself." Ellie nodded as she pursed her lips. "When I pushed him to explain that, he said that maybe it's not so much that Marcus isn't himself, but more that the real Marcus no longer wants to be in his old life."

My heart soared at that. But I tamped it down. "I don't want him miserable just so *I* can get my dream."

"You did the right thing and now you just have to be patient. Not to sound trite, but you know the old saying *If you love someone, let them go. If they come back, they were always yours.*"

I scoffed. "Don't you think I don't know the rest of that little saying."

Ellie rolled her eyes and waved away my pity party. "Don't *you* think I didn't see the love between you. Sometimes a person—or a couple—has to experience the worst of times to be able to better appreciate the best of times."

"I want to go see him," I ventured.

"So, go see him. You've got three very capable people to help with the farm."

"The city makes me nervous. I've only been there once or twice. The first time, with my parents, we got a flat tire and the whole trip was rife with tension and stress. The second time, I got lost and never did find the location of the meeting I was supposed to attend. I gave up going to Rockhurst after that. If I can't get it in Kingsley or Shilesville or another nearby town, I'll order it online or go without." I sipped my coffee. "But I miss him so damn much. Kinda wanted to surprise him with a visit."

"Is the anxiety of the city the only thing that's stopping you?"

I bit my lip and took a deep breath. "What if I get there and see that he's so much happier with his city life than he was with me?"

"Hogwash," Ellie exclaimed. "You've already said he seems as miserable as you do. But I think it best to give him a bit of a head's up so he doesn't make plans out of boredom. Let him have time to set up a good weekend for you." She patted my hand. "And you'll take my car. That big truck of yours would make city driving—especially the parking—a real bear."

After helping Ellie clean up, we did a walk-through of the BnB both inside and out to see what needed repairs or updating. When only one job made it onto my list, I knew I'd been given the gift of time. Ms. Bethany and Scott could handle the farm for three and a half days. I'd leave on Thursday after morning chores and return Sunday night.

That night, after busting ass all day to complete the BnB job, finish every single open order, and do the evening chores, I showered and ate a dinner of leftovers thanks to Ellie. When my phone buzzed with a text from Marc suggesting a video chat, I couldn't wipe the smile from my face.

When a very tired-looking, but at least smiling Marc appeared on my computer screen, I blurted, "I want to come visit!"

His eyes went wide. "Yes, definitely. When? Name the time."

"Thursday? Around noon? Stay until Sunday?" Then a thought hit me. "Oh, shit. I didn't even think about your work. Can you take off?"

"I'll get everything done tonight, tomorrow, and Thursday morning. No worries. Thursday by noon, I'll be all yours."

Marc's eyes danced and my heart soared to see that he appeared to be as happy as I felt.

"So, I taught you all about the country. It's time for the city boy to take me to school," I teased.

"Oxford at your service." His smile broadened. "Damn, I can't believe how excited I am about this. What do you want to do?"

"I'll leave it up to you. I have massive anxiety about the city—Ellie wants me to drive her car to avoid the hassle of parking my truck—so you can be in charge of showing me what you think I need to experience."

"Perfect. I'll make a list and set it all up."

We talked for a little longer. Marc's eyes dimming each time he spoke of his father and work—the meetings, clients, and big sales he used to seem to get so excited about appeared to be bringing him nothing but tension and stress now. But when I filled him in on the chickens, the BnB, the orders that continued to pour in, and the veggie haul I'd made that day, he perked up as if a weight had been taken off his shoulders.

"Well, Hank will crow at the ass-crack of dawn," I said with a laugh. "I should be heading to bed."

"I miss Hank." Marc frowned. "I can't believe I miss a damn noisy-ass rooster."

We said our goodbye's and disconnected.

I settled into bed with a happy heart. There was work to do before I could leave, but in less than forty-eight hours, I'd be with Marc again.

∿

THE LADY on my GPS indicated I'd arrived at my destination. Grateful to be pulling Ellie's smaller car into the parking garage—I didn't think my truck would have made the turn—I gave the gate attendant my name.

"Jordan Moore. I'm a guest of Marcus Kingsley." Dread shot through me. What if he'd forgotten to give the parking attendant my name? What if I was holding up traffic? What if I had to back up and go home? My already-sweaty palms felt as if they were soaking the steering wheel.

"There you are," the lady smiled kindly as she checked her list. "Mr. Kingsley's guest spot is on the third level. Row B, spot seven. You'll park right next to him. Here's your pass. Hang it on your mirror. Enjoy your stay."

I took the pass, said thank you, and didn't breathe again until I was parked in spot seven next to Marc's car. Wiping my sweaty palms on my pants, I took a long, ragged breath. I had four days to spend with my guy and I wasn't going to waste them being sweaty and nervous. Or at least I was going to do my best.

I'd shared my location with Marc so he could track my arrival. Which meant once I climbed from the car, I was greeted by his smile, a long hug, and a tender kiss filled with promise.

"Oh my God, I can't believe you're really here," Marc whispered against my lips.

I fought the urge to glance around to be sure we were alone and smiled. "I can't either. Maybe I can relax a bit now that I've got my own city guide." I kissed him again.

I pulled my bag from the backseat and winced when I saw the shirt I'd hung from the hook. "I kinda freaked out packing. I realized I'd probably need nicer clothes here, but I don't really have any. I packed my black jeans and black work boots and that shirt. But I'm sure I'll stick out like a sore thumb." The heart palpitations had returned—and not because of being back with Marc.

"No worries. I actually have a solution for that." He tugged my hand toward the elevator. "How was the drive?"

"Not bad. I didn't have any issues until I reached Rockhurst. I missed one exit and had to wait for GPS to recalibrate. I hate downtown driving; what's with all the one-way streets?" My eyes went wide as we entered the sparkling glass elevator. The view of the city was impressive even if a little dizzying.

"No driving until you have to leave. We'll walk or call an Uber. Hell, we might even do a taxi so you can experience that." He pulled me close and kissed me again. "Sorry if I'm too clingy. I feel like I've got time to make up for."

"Not at all. I'd prefer to keep in close contact the entire time I'm here."

The elevator stopped and we walked out to a little alcove with three doors.

"These are the best three apartments in the building. This one is mine." He gestured toward a door.

After unlocking the door with a fancy key-fob, Marc ushered me inside.

The space was large, open, and sleek. Immaculate, deluxe, impressive…the words kept piling up in my head as I took in the apartment. Gorgeous for sure, but there was something more. Sterile. Sparse. Hauntingly empty and alone. Oh, not that the space was empty. Marc had decorated—or likely had someone decorate—in a very modern feel. But the whole place felt as if it was just a model, a mask, a persona to hide behind.

"Wow, nice place," I said. My heart clenching to think of Marc here alone night after night.

"Eh, it's pretty to look at."

"But?" I prodded as I dropped my bag.

"I've realized lately just how lonely and cold this place is." He reached for me and hugged me close as my heart broke for him. "I don't *live* here. I exist here. It's not the real me and I'm beginning to hate it here," he whispered.

"Well, I'm here for now. Show me around," I said. When what I really wanted to say was *Let's just leave. We'll go back to Kingsley. You never have to stay here again.*

After a tour of the large apartment—in which I kept my mouth shut, but wondered what in the hell one person needed with so much space—Marc asked if I wanted to get lunch.

"I'm starving," I agreed.

We had food delivered. Marc swore the deli he ordered from was the best in the city, and I had to agree that the food was fantastic. The delivery charge was crazy to me and made me laugh, but we spread out on the floor at the sleek, modern coffee table—which looked as if it had never once had an actual cup of coffee placed on it—and tore into our food.

"So, I've got a couple things on our list of must-do's." Marc's eyes danced with excitement.

"I'm ready, hit me."

"Sushi," he began and then laughed. "Stop looking like that. I swear, it's not all raw and you'll love it."

I wrinkled my nose. "If you say so. Can we at least have a box of cereal and milk ready for later when I'm inevitably hungry because I can't stomach any of the sushi?"

Marc laughed. "Yes, we'll place a grocery order."

"That seems excessive, but city boy knows best." I winked.

"I was able to find two Broadway shows playing and thought we'd hit the theater a couple times. One is playing an afternoon performance on Saturday and one is Friday night. Falsettos and Miss Saigon. You can't come to the city and not watch a show—I mean, we're not in New York for actual on-Broadway productions, but the theater talent around here is really quite good."

I shrugged. "I've never really been a fan of musicals, but I'll go." I winced. "How dressy are we talking?"

"Ah, so that's what I took care of." He pulled me to my feet. "I knew if I asked you to bring something dressy, you'd freak out because you don't really have any need for *dressy*. So, I got you a pair of pants, two shirts, and shoes. We won't need ties."

I frowned. "So, you're saying my country clothes aren't good enough for your city activities."

Marc's eyes narrowed. "No, I'm saying I knew you'd freak out and then likely feel uncomfortable in anything you brought to wear. I would have just let you wear my clothes, but we both know the fit would have left you in highwater pants. Are you mad?"

For a split-second, I wanted to be. I wanted to be offended. But Marc was right. None of my clothes were right for going to the theater. He would have told me I was fine in my black jeans, black work boots, and button-down, but I would have felt out of place all night. I smiled softly. "No. I'm touched that you went to the trouble to make me feel comfortable."

He let out a breath. "Oh good. You had me worried for a moment." He led me to the closet in his room and gestured to the clothing and shoes he'd gotten me. "You can even leave them here if you'd like."

While I wanted to say I had high hopes he wouldn't be here much longer, I knew that was selfish. "Yeah, that's probably the best plan."

I surveyed his room, my eyes landing on his dresser. Walking closer, I ran my hand over the birdhouse with a sad smile. "It doesn't really fit the place does it?"

Marc came to stand behind me. "No, it doesn't. I'm

beginning to think the birdhouse and I have a lot in common."

We stood, wrapped in each other's arms, for several moments. Just breathing each other in, reacclimating our bodies, savoring the closeness.

"So, what's on the agenda for today?" I asked.

"Would you be terribly disappointed if I said I only made plans for today that included the bedroom and maybe the shower?" Marc grinned.

"Not disappointed at all." I kissed him and took hold of the loosened tie he still wore from his morning at work. "In fact, I think I'd very much like to get my Oxford out of his stuffy city boy clothes and into bed."

"That can totally be arranged." Marc kissed me, sliding his tongue between my lips.

We spent the rest of the day in bed. After two rounds of hot, sweaty sex, we took a shower, ordered food, and settled in to watch a movie. Exhaustion finally took over and we slept—with a middle-of-the-night round three—and woke happy and sated in each other's arms when the sun came through the windows.

"This is nice," Marc murmured.

"Mmm," I moaned.

"But it's missing something," he said.

"Missing what?"

"I don't know. I love you and I love having you here. But I still feel like something is incomplete." He pressed a kiss against my temple.

"We're together, that's all that matters," I said. But I knew exactly what he meant. I felt it, too.

MARC TOOK me to the office and introduced me to his sister. Ed Kingsley was also there and I got a chance to visit with him for a while. He and I laughed about Ellie's spunk and the way people flocked to the BnB just for the chance to meet her.

"That new internet she got sure does make a world of difference. A few years back, the lack of connection was my one big reason for staying in the city instead of packing up and moving to Kingsley permanently." Ed leaned back in his chair as we chatted comfortably in his office.

"From what Marc says," Marissa chimed in, "he didn't even notice a single bit of change from his service here in the city. Gramps, you should think about making that move."

"Believe me, it's a top consideration." Ed smiled. "Just a few things here I need to solidify."

We went on to talk about our plans for the weekend. Marissa suggested she and her husband could get a babysitter and come out with us, but the look Marc shot her silenced that idea.

She smiled with a wink. "So, yeah. Seems like maybe you boys have your weekend all planned. Maybe we could all come visit and stay at the BnB one weekend." Marissa eyed her brother suspiciously. "Marc insists that Kingsley is heaven on earth."

"I didn't say that," Marc grumbled.

"Well, the way you get all floaty and sappy when you talk about Jordan and the town makes it seem that way," Marissa teased.

Marc blushed.

My heart did that funny flip-flop thing. Being with Marc had me feeling like a teen in love again—although, I'd never actually been a teen in love. He'd given me so many things that I'd missed out on in my younger days.

"I told you." Ed smiled triumphantly. "It's a good thing

you threw yourself under the bus for your sister and earned three months away rather than two."

"Thanks for that, by the way." Marissa blushed. "I screwed up, but I shouldn't have let you take the fall."

Marc shrugged. "No big deal. Dad's perpetually disappointed in me. I was going away for an extended amount of time. Better the heat be on me than on you."

"Well, she fessed up pretty quickly—guilt got to her I think—and we spent about a week making it right. All good now." Ed's eyes narrowed as he studied Marc's hand clasping mine. "Speaking of my son, have you seen your father today?"

Marc bristled. "No. Not really planning on it. Part of me wants to just to throw in his face how happy I am." He squeezed my hand. "Make him see that his opinion doesn't matter. But mostly I just want to avoid the asshole."

"I really don't see why you keep working here," Marissa said. "You hate working for Dad. You could get a job anywhere."

My heart picked up speed. The conversation was bordering on awkward—like the type where you feel like you probably shouldn't be hearing it, but it's happening anyway.

"It's the family business. I work here for Gramps and Gran." Marc shrugged. "But I'm off right now, so we're going to head out. We've got sights to see and city stuff to experience. Dinner and a show tonight." He stood and pulled me with him.

"Have fun. What are you seeing?" Marissa asked.

I squinted my eyes. "Tonight, I think, is Miss Saigon? Tomorrow, Falsettos."

Ed coughed. "Damn, Marcus. Couldn't find some more cheerful shows?"

Marc winced. "Short notice. These are *good* productions."

Marissa patted my arm. "Take tissues."

After our goodbyes, Marc took my hand as we walked toward the elevator. I'd quickly started to adore how he seemed to want to take my hand at all times. And I wondered how it would play out if we held hands in public back in Kingsley.

"So, you're taking me to sad theater shows?" I bumped my shoulder against his.

"I mean," he started, but then hesitated, "we don't have to go. I just wanted you to get the theater experience."

I squeezed his hand. "My theater experience mostly consists of year-old movies or a sheet on the side of my shed. I'm happy to expand my horizons with Broadway shows. But if I cry, you don't get to make fun of me."

"You'll likely cry...or at least get choked up. They are *very* different shows, but both are emotional for sure." He gave me a quick kiss right before the elevator opened. "Definitely no judgement. In fact, if you *don't* get a little teary, I may wonder what's wrong with you."

We spent the rest of the day exploring the city, eating lunch at one of Marc's favorite burger joints, taking a wild taxi ride—which Marc promised had been one of the most laid-back cab rides he'd ever experienced—and shopping at some touristy places.

Marc laughed as we left a store. "I've never even been in that store. But all the people who come to visit always make a beeline for it."

"I guess I'm a true tourist—do I stick out that badly?"

He wrapped an arm around my shoulder. "You're not a tourist. You're a visitor and you're with me—a certified city boy—so it's all good."

We ended up back at his place in the late afternoon to nap, shower, and get ready for our evening.

"Is this kinda like our first date?" I teased.

Marc cocked his head. "I don't know. Do we count the river?"

We both laughed.

"But seriously, I guess maybe this is our first city date, but definitely not our first date. The river, shopping, Candle Light Diner, the movie, sleeping in your truck, the field party, all of those count as dates to me." He stepped close to me and brushed his lips over my ear. "City or country, fancy or just a normal day, being with you is always a special occasion."

"My Oxford is such a smooth talker," I murmured.

We stripped to our underwear under the premise of taking a nap. We *did* eventually sleep, but other, more pertinent activities, took place first.

DINNER WAS at a cute little hole-in-the-wall Mexican place with the best chips and salsa I'd ever tasted in my life. Marc ordered some huge sampler platter and we shared. Every single bite I put in my mouth was better than the last.

"It's not bread and gravy or sweet corn," Marc pouted, "but it's pretty good."

"I'd definitely drive to Rockhurst just for this place," I assured him. "Kingsley is sorely lacking in the Mexican food department. This is amazing."

"We can make it our usual place when you come to visit," Marc assured.

Passing up dessert because we were stuffed, we headed to the register to pay.

"I can get my own," I started to pull out my wallet.

"Nope, you paid for a lot on your turf. Now it's my turn." Marc handed over his card.

On the way out the door, he took my hand. "Did I tell you how amazing you look tonight?"

My cheeks heated. "Once or twice."

"Well, I'll never stop loving you in work clothes—even camo has its place in my heart now," he teased with a bump of his hip against mine. "But seeing you dressed up is a treat in itself."

"I still love the image of your ass in a pair of jeans." I gave his hand a squeeze. "But there's definitely something sexy as hell about you in dress clothes."

We continued our mutual admiration and teasing banter as we headed toward the theater.

One thing I appreciated about walking everywhere in the city was the fact it allowed me to walk off the heavy meal before we settled into our seats for Miss Saigon. The theater boasted its history in the architecture and ambience, but spoke of its ability to provide the most spectacular shows through its technology, performers, and amenities. Sitting with Marc, his hand clasping mine as the lights went down—knowing I was experiencing my first live theater show with the man I loved—brought on a heavy warm feeling that had nothing to do with the huge meal we'd just consumed.

After over two hours of watching some of the most talented performers I'd ever seen—better than some of the biggest names in Hollywood, I swore they were—the curtain fell and I most definitely had to wipe tears from my eyes.

Marc squeezed my hand. "Told you. But it was good, right?"

I nodded as we stood to exit the theater. "Very good. Gut-wrenching. I mean, I guess one can't assume a production about the Vietnam war is going to be all happy and shit. But damn, that ending. And those *voices* were absolutely amazing," I chatted quietly as we made our way outside. I ran my thumb over the back of his hand. "Thank you for that. It's not something I ever would have picked for myself—thinking I didn't like musicals—but that was really enjoyable. Even if I did cry."

"Tomorrow's show is completely different in topic and feel, but you'll likely still need your tissues." Marc paused as we were walking. "I can't believe I'm going to do this. But I think you need to experience the city's public transport."

We ended up laughing our asses off as we took two wrong buses and eventually had to call an Uber to get us back to Marc's place.

"Okay, so I've maybe never had to take the bus and it's probably a good thing. I really didn't realize it was that difficult." Marc chuckled as he swiped his key to open the apartment door. "How do people do that every day? I'd be doubly stressed."

"Probably like anything else. Difficult until you get practice and then it becomes simple."

We ended up in the bedroom, stripping our clothes in preparation for a shower.

"Can I tell you something?" I asked. I'd brought something along with me—could have probably just kept it hidden and Marc would have never known—but my original plan had been eating at me.

Marc paused and nodded. "Nothing bad?"

"No. And I don't even really know why I'm bringing it up." I shrugged. Heat filling my face, I grabbed my bag and pulled out the dildo—still in its box—that I'd purchased a week ago. "I brought this thinking we'd use it and I'd bottom for you. But…"

Marc shook his head. "No. I want that. I do. But it's not for here. When I take you, I want to be in our bed on the farm. I love having you here, but it's not where I want that to happen for the first time."

I let out a sigh of relief as my heart smiled at the way Marc referred to *our bed*. "Feels good to know you get it. I'm loving every second of being with you, but it all kinda feels like we're acting or going through motions. I want to bottom, but if we did it here, it would almost feel like just checking a box."

"I get it one hundred percent." Marc wrapped me in his arms. "*However*," he purred, "I could completely get behind a shower and then you using one of *my* toys on me."

We made our way through prep and showers before falling onto Marc's bed in a hot, damp tangle of limbs.

Even without the *need* to stretch him with fingers and tongue—he swore the toy would be enough—I never tired of the clench of his tight ring on my fingers or the taste of him on my tongue as I teased his body open.

When Marc was writhing under my touch, I lubed the silicone toy. "I've never done this, tell me if I'm doing it wrong," I mumbled.

"The only thing *wrong* will be if you make me come before you get your dick in me," Marc panted as he pulled his knees back to give me more of his hole.

"Good to know." I split my attention between his face and his entrance. While I'd always love watching his body open for my fingers, my tongue, my cock, there was definitely something sexy about watching him take the toy. And the look on his face—a mix of adjusting to and blissing out over the intrusion—was enough to spur me on.

I stroked my dick as I slid the silicone in and out of Marc's tight hole.

"God, that's good, but I've gotten spoiled by having the real thing day and night." He gasped as I shifted the angle and pegged him just right.

"Is it weird that I'm slightly jealous of a dildo?"

Marc chuckled. "It's served its purpose. I'm ready for you —would have been ready without it, but that was fun.

Another *city experience* to add to your list. But I want you in me. Now."

Not needing any convincing, I slid the toy gently from his body before slicking my cock. Kneeling between his knees, I pressed the head of my cock against his hole and groaned as he opened for me. One long thrust and I was balls deep, shifting forward to take him in my arms as his legs wrapped around my waist.

That night wasn't about hard and fast. I held him in my arms and pumped slowly, making sure he knew how much I loved him. When my orgasm began to tease, I refused to rush. When Marc began to beg, I refused to increase the speed.

Knowing he was close, I went deeper with each slow thrust until Marc was groaning under me. His orgasm erupted between us, his ass clenching my shaft, as his fingers dug into the sweaty skin on my back.

With one last, long pump of my hips, I found my release. Wave after wave of delicious heat washed over my body as my cock pulsed deep in Marc's body.

We took what seemed like forever to regain our senses. Even when my softening cock slipped from his body, we stayed wrapped together. "That was almost more than words can explain," I murmured against his neck.

"Agreed." Marc ran his hands up and down my back. "While the city may not feel like home, we'll always have *that* as the best memory of being here." He tipped my chin and kissed me tenderly. "I love you. So damn much."

"Love you," I whispered. "More than I can explain."

"Think you did a pretty good job showing me," he teased with a delicious moan and wiggle of his hips.

After a quick clean up, we settled in to sleep.

"Do you think, if I was able to stay here for three months,

that I'd ever come to feel about Rockhurst like you do about Kingsley?" I asked.

Marc was quiet for a moment. "Maybe? But honestly, I think the way I feel about Kingsley has more to do with you and Gran—and the way you both love the place so much. The fact that I'm beginning to feel pretty apathetic for the city makes me think that you could be happy to be here with me, but likely never *love* the place because I no longer love it."

"I can see that." His thinking made sense. "I wish there was a way to fix our issue. I hate the thought of you being miserable here."

"We'll make it work. I can deal with miserable here if it means having you here from time-to-time and visits to Kingsley." Marc curled into my chest. "I'm already looking forward to next weekend."

WE EXITED the theater into the bright and unseasonably cool June afternoon. The cool weather wasn't the best for my veggies back home, but it made walking around in the unfamiliar dress pants and dress shirt a bit more comfortable.

"What'd you think?" Marc asked as we waited at a crosswalk.

"That was amazing." My cheeks still felt damp from the tears I'd shed at the end of Falsettos. "I guess the ending shouldn't have taken me by surprise—the time period was enough of a clue—but it wasn't until a certain point that I even began to suspect. And then, even though I was still caught up in the performance, I was filled with a sadness about what I knew was coming. And it's kinda a cliffhanger in a way. Makes you have to predict what happened after."

"Yeah, I've always thought that show was a strange mix of

funny and sad." He opened the door to the sushi restaurant he'd promised I'd love.

"What other productions should I watch?" I glanced around the place and relaxed a bit. The aroma of food made my stomach growl and the atmosphere put me at ease—not sure what I'd been expecting, but I'd had it all wrong in my head; the place seemed great. Surely, I could at least get some noodles or something while Marc enjoyed his sushi.

"Wicked is a must. I think it's coming back next year. And you'd love Hamilton. We definitely have to get tickets to that. I watched it when it was available on-line, but I would love to see a live production." Marc settled in beside me at the tiny corner booth.

The space was the perfect almost-private, cozy spot and I already loved the restaurant and the memory we were building even if I wouldn't eat ninety-nine percent of what was on the menu.

"Can I get Coke or do they not serve that?" I asked quietly.

Marc bit back a smile. "They have Coke."

When the waitperson arrived, we gave our drink orders and asked for a bit of time to decide on our food order.

"Are you going to be mad if I order just noodles?" I winced.

Marc placed a warm hand on my knee. "I'm not going to be *mad* about it; order what you want. But can I place a sushi order with both of us in mind and you'll at least try it?"

I grimaced. "Promise nothing raw?"

"Promise. I *can* eat the raw stuff, but I enjoy the cooked better." He slid one of the menus my way. "I'll order *only* from the cooked choices."

I gave a nod as I scanned the menu for noodles. "Okay, I'll at least try it. But don't order too much; I may try like two pieces. I guess you could take it home?"

When the waitperson returned with our drinks, I requested an order of noodles. Marc ordered about ten different items and my eyes bugged as I added up the cost in my head.

"You just ordered nearly seventy-five dollars worth of food that only you are going to eat," I whispered.

Marc chuckled. "I wanted to get things I thought you'd like. If this was the all-you-can-eat type place, we wouldn't be able to take extras home. But I can always ask for a box later; I'd say it could be my lunch on Monday, but I doubt the leftovers will make it through Sunday." He rubbed my thigh. "I'll be drowning myself in my sorrows by Sunday night; shoving my face with sushi seems like the perfect way to stop missing my boyfriend."

I pretended to be shocked. "I'm so easy to get over that a shit-ton of sushi will ease your sadness?"

"Not in the least bit," Marc replied seriously, "but at least I can enjoy a delicious treat while I cry over you leaving."

"I can't believe how much food you ordered," I mused. "And is sushi always that pricey?"

Marc shrugged. "All-you-can-eat places are a bit more affordable in that you can order a lot of different items for the cost, but any *cheap* sushi place should be approached with caution. There's this little place outside of the city that used to be a Pizza Hut—probably before I was even born—and it's now a sushi place. I'd seen it a couple times and thought *no way*, but a friend had been and swore it was amazing. We went for lunch one day and it was really good." He took a sip of his drink. "There's a lot of effort and talent that goes into putting the sushi rolls together. I think you'll love the presentation. And that's how they get you; they offer so many amazing options that you want to try some of everything and, before you know it, you've got a tray the size of your table arriving."

As if on cue, the smiling waitperson descended on us with a tray of beautifully created rolls of sushi. The server sat the tray down, explained which roll was which, and walked away.

"It really is gorgeous. The use of color and textures is amazing. Who knew food could be so beautiful?" I took my bowl of noodles from the tray.

"Oh, I don't know, have you ever seen a plate full of bread and gravy accented with sweet corn-on-the-cob slathered in butter and sprinkled with salt?" Marc winked. "I need to let Gran know I'm coming next weekend and put in my request for my new favorite meal."

I took a bite of noodles; they were delicious. The Chinese place in Kingsley had good food, no doubt. But these noodles were just as tasty.

"Okay, I want you to try four pieces," Marc began.

"Four!?"

"You don't even have to eat the whole piece, just a bite. A *bite* of four different pieces. I won't be mad if you don't like it, but knowing what I know of your food likes and dislikes, I really do think you'll love it."

I narrowed my eyes at him. "Only because I love you and trust you."

Marc put four pieces of sushi on my plate. "Nothing raw, promise. This one is shrimp." He pointed to the one in the twelve o'clock position. "Then chicken, spicy crab, and lobster, crab mixture." He indicated each roll in a clockwise pattern. "They all have rice, a thin seaweed wrap, and various toppings of different sauces and crunchy pieces."

"Different sauces and crunchy pieces sounds very technical," I teased as I eyed the four round pieces on my plate. "Okay, here goes. If I'm throwing up tonight, I'm blaming you."

My eyes went wide as I chewed the bite. The different textures—which I would have thought could never go together—mixed perfectly. The blend of flavors—just the right fusion of bland rice, savory meat, and spicy sauce—danced on my tongue.

Marc waited, his eyes never leaving my face.

I swallowed. "Okay, okay. The shrimp one was amazing. Save me a piece of that one." I went on to try the other three rolls and could have fallen out of my seat with shock at how much I loved the flavors. "I'll be damned," I muttered after the last bite.

Marc smiled broadly, like a proud parent who'd just taught his kid how to ride a bike. "So, you like it?"

I took a drink and nodded. "I never mind admitting I'm wrong or that you're right, but I wouldn't have predicted this outcome in a million years. As long as you are here to order for me, I'll eat sushi with you anytime."

"So, no throwing up tonight?" he teased.

"Only if I end up eating too much." I eyed the tray. "Which I'm guessing could easily happen."

"Oh well, if there are no leftovers, I'll drown my sorrows in ice cream instead."

"I want there to be leftovers. I'm thinking a sushi breakfast in bed should become one of our Sunday routines when I'm here." I caressed his leg and reached for more sushi.

We ended up with about ten pieces leftover and Marc asked for a box before paying the ridiculous bill and leaving a generous tip.

"This weekend has been amazing. As much as I loved showing you the ropes in the country, I loved being with you in the city just as much." I took his hand as we walked toward his apartment.

Marc eyed our joined hands with a wistful smile. "But you'd still rather spend our time together in Kingsley, right?"

"Well, yeah. That's where I'm most comfortable and feel

at home. But, seriously, as long as I'm with you, I can deal with wherever we are." I shrugged. "After this weekend, at least I know that trips to the city won't be as stressful as my mind had painted them to be."

"If I ever get my choice, we'll always be together in Kingsley. We can visit the city together." Marc led me into the elevator and pulled me against his chest as we ascended to his floor.

THIRTEEN

MARC

JORDAN and I had fallen into a comfortable routine after two months of living in separate locations. Daily texts, nightly video chats, and a couple of every other weekend visits.

I'd been back to Kingsley two times. We hadn't had a chance for Jordan to bottom; one weekend I was there, his sister and her kids came to visit. The other weekend I was at the farm, we'd both been dealing with a head cold; we spent most of our time slogging through chores, taking cold medicine, sipping tea, and sleeping.

But I'd still loved every single moment of my time in the small town.

Jordan had managed to visit the city twice more since his first weekend trip; his weekends in Rockhurst were amazing and I loved building memories with him.

But Rockhurst wasn't where I wanted to be.

Certified city boy that I swore I'd always be continued to pine away for Kingsley.

Yes, the way my heart yearned for that small country blip on the map had most everything to do with Jordan; I'd honestly probably feel a pull toward any location where he was. But Kingsley was where Jordan lived, where his life and heart belonged. So, Kingsley was where my heart wanted to be.

Instead, I was stuck sitting through another boring meeting. My head pounding as it seemed to do every damn day I walked into the office. My stomach churning over the report my team was preparing to give next on the agenda. And my mind trudging through a heavy blanket of wet sludge as I resigned myself to *this* being my life.

When had I stopped loving the high-energy, tension-filled world of sales management?

When you slowed down long enough to realize there was more to life.

When had I stopped loving the bright city lights and constant nightlife?

When you found the quiet peace of Jordan's arms.

When had my apartment started to feel like a mausoleum, closing in on me and stealing my breath with each passing day?

When you experienced the comfortable coziness of spending time in an old farmhouse with the man you love.

"Marcus?" my father's voice boomed.

I jerked from my thoughts.

Somehow, mostly thanks to my team, I made it through the report presentation. My father spent the entire time looking bored and disappointed. I wasn't sure if I'd ever seen my father look at me in any other way. That fact used to bring me sadness and the feeling that I *had* to do better, be better, finally find a way to make him proud.

But now? There was no winning with my father. No matter how good I did, how hard I worked, it was never enough. And I'd come to believe that was a lot more about him than about me. The man was filled with too much pain, anger, and deeply hidden emotional turmoil for me to ever break through. Honestly, it wasn't my place. Since coming home from Kingsley, I'd decided that my dad needed professional help, but he wasn't my responsibility. I was no longer going to waste my mental and emotional energy on him.

Without so much as a word, Dad stalked from the room after the meeting.

Gramps stayed in his usual chair at the head of the conference table. "That was very good. As always. Thorough, promising, and something for other teams to strive toward."

I smiled sadly. "Thanks. At least I'm good for something." Telling myself to forget about my father was one thing. Actually convincing myself that what he thought of me wasn't right would take a bit more doing.

Gramps frowned. "Close the door, Marc."

I glanced around and noticed we were alone in the room. Somewhat curious and at least a bit concerned, I closed the door and took a seat near Gramps. Not my father's chair, but close to it.

"I wanted you to be the first to know—well, aside from Ellie, of course." Gramps scribbled something on a paper and closed the leather-bound portfolio in front of him. "I'm making a permanent move to Kingsley."

My jaw dropped. "And leaving the company to Dad?"

Gramps shrugged. "I'll still be part of it in name and the shares I own. While you were away, we sent out a client satisfaction survey. It's something we've done several times before, but this time the answers meant more to me. In the past, I've used the answers to prove that I had a responsibility to stay. Now? The answers showed me that our clients are happy despite my son being a grade-A asshole."

I chuckled. "They clearly don't know Marcus Kingsley, Sr. the way you and I do."

"Exactly. But that's my point. I've been giving more and

more of the day-to-day operations and big-picture stuff to your dad over the past couple years. As much as he's a jerk in his personal life, he's excelled at the business life. Clients don't know that he's an asshole. And I'm not sure they'd care as long as they're getting the service they've come to expect from our company." Gramps smiled. "And the survey proves they are. So, I feel comfortable stepping down in all but name and shares only. I'll still be part of big decisions and available for day-to-day stuff for a while, but I'll also be happily running a BnB with my dear Ellie."

"Wait, if you'll be there permanently, does that mean the BnB will be a year-long thing? I know Gran would love that." My heart warmed thinking of how much Gran would love a crackling fire in the hearth, warm mugs of hot chocolate, and something delicious baking as the snow fell outside.

"We've been discussing it. Our options are to keep it open all year long or keep the schedule as it is and head to Florida during the winter months. Gran seems to be torn fifty-fifty right now."

"I'm so happy for you." And I truly was. My grandparents deserved their dreams. "Gotta admit I'm pretty jealous, too." I smiled sheepishly.

"Kingsley got to you, huh?" Gramps smiled knowingly.

"Yeah, it did. But..." The words caught in my throat.

"But Jordan got to you even more?"

I nodded as tears stung my eyes. "Never thought I'd sit in this office that I love so much and say that I would happily leave and never look back if given a chance." I shrugged. "But that's where I'm at."

Gramps cocked his head with a scowl. "So leave."

My eyes shot to his. "I can't. This is my job. It's the family business. I have a responsibility."

He rolled his eyes. "We live in a virtual world now, son. I've been traveling to Kingsley long enough to know that telecommuting to business meetings works just as well as sitting in this stuffy ol' office. You have state-of-the-art hardware and software, reliable internet access, and a phone; you can do your part of the business from anywhere."

My heart skipped a beat and then rushed to catch up. "For real?"

"You've built a kick-ass team that you trust completely. Your position doesn't require in-person, on-site work. Same as me. If I did it, why can't you?"

"Yeah, but you did it for a few days to a week at a time, not permanently." I worried my bottom lip.

"I'm doing it permanently now."

"And stepping away from a lot of the day-to-day. What if I can't keep up?"

Gramps scoffed. "Nonsense. You're one of the best, most efficient, top-notch managers we've got." He quirked a brow. "And if you try it and it doesn't work, maybe you say goodbye to the business. I'm a firm believer in doing what makes you happy. You've been back here almost three months and I swear—with the exception of the smiles you get when Jordan comes to visit—you're back to being as bad off mentally and physically as you were before Kingsley. Don't stay stuck in something that makes you miserable."

I nodded and stood. "I'll think about it."

When I reached the door, my head a swirl of emotions and doubts and crazy ideas, Gramps said my name.

"I'm leaving today to go to Kingsley for a visit—I'll take care of the permanent move stuff in a week or so. I'd be happy to give you a ride. That car of yours isn't made for country living; sell it and get something more appropriate. Or use that boy's truck or Gran's car." Gramps smiled, his eyes dancing wildly. "You don't have to have all the answers right now. But I'm leaving in a couple hours if you want to take a road trip with an old man."

My head swam with possibilities and uncertainties. But I nodded. "I'll think about it."

"Two hours. Be at my place if you want to go." Gramps winked.

I left the conference room and went to my office.

On autopilot, I gathered my computer and its accessories. I passed Marissa in the hallway.

"Where are you going?" She frowned.

"Home," I answered. I didn't have the mental capacity to explain at that exact moment; I wasn't even sure I completely knew exactly what I was doing. "I'll talk to you more about it later."

Thirty minutes later—after robotically emptying my fridge, cleaning the bathroom and kitchen, and taking out the trash—I stood at the door to my apartment with a large duffel bag and the birdhouse in my arms. Without a single shred of sadness or regret, I gave a nod to the place and shut the door. I wasn't at all sure of what was next, but I knew in my heart that I was doing the right thing.

I arrived at Gramps' place an hour early.

He looked up from throwing a bag in the trunk and smiled as I walked up his driveway. "Here I thought I'd have to wait until the final moment to see if you'd show up. Ready to roll?"

"What about my apartment?" I asked in a daze.

"Pff, that thing will sell in a heartbeat." Gramps eyed me. "You sure about this? I don't want to talk you into something you don't really want. I guess I just thought…"

"Take me home," I said as a smile spread across my face. I tossed my bag into the trunk, sat the birdhouse on the floorboard, and climbed in. The anxiety and dread I'd been living with over the last nearly three months lifted as I settled in for the most important two-hour drive of my life.

"KNOW any country boys who might want to take a city slicker to lunch?" I asked with a broad smile on my face as I poked my head into Jordan's office at the back of the house.

He startled from the paperwork he'd been doing but broke into a huge grin when he saw me. Rushing from his chair behind the desk, he wrapped me in a warm embrace and kissed me as if having me there was the answer to all of his problems.

When we finally broke apart, he cupped my face. "How are you here? I thought I had to wait at least another week."

"I can leave," I offered with a teasing smile and started to back away.

He grabbed me and pulled me close. "No way. I'm thrilled you're here. The next couple days just got a whole lot better."

"I'm not interrupting anything?" Suddenly, anxiety washed over me. What the hell was I thinking? Did I just expect Jordan would accept me moving to Kingsley for good? Could I stay with him? Would I need to find my own place?

"Not at all. I was going to eat lunch with Ellie in a bit. We can eat there or go into town."

"Perfect. I hope she fixed enough. Gramps drove me. He was coming to visit and I decided I'd come too." I decided I'd let the weekend play out and see how I felt on Sunday before telling Jordan I was thinking about moving to town permanently.

Jordan rushed to finish his paperwork before lunch and I texted Gramps to let him know I wasn't telling anyone else about my possible decision just yet.

As we walked the backway through the pastures and fields to get to Gran's, Jordan took my hand. "You have no idea how happy I am to have you here. I wasn't doing anything special this weekend, but having you here makes it seem like I've got something amazing planned."

After a laughter-filled lunch with Jordan, Gramps, and Gran, we walked the BnB property to pick up sticks and check for repairs. Then we said goodbye and headed back to the farm.

The rest of the day was spent doing chores, working in the shop, and laughing. That night, we watched a movie in the back of Jordan's truck and had our own little Marc-approved type of campout—which of course meant not on the ground.

Saturday dawned stormy so we waited as long as we could to do the chores, but ended up picking veggies and gathering eggs in a downpour. Then I made several birdhouses while Jordan finished up three orders in the shop. Dinner with Gramps and Gran rounded out our evening and we headed home after pie and coffee.

"Shower?" I suggested when we kicked off our shoes in the mudroom at Jordan's house.

He snaked his arms around my neck and bit his lip; his eyes searching mine in the moonlight. "Separate? Give me a bit of time to prep?"

My cock immediately jumped on board with the idea and I whispered, "Fuck yes," before kissing him. "But I'll do the same because there's every chance I'll blow within sixty-seconds, so we may need to flip."

I had Jordan naked by the time we reached the bathroom. "Take all the time you need. Then, I want you naked on the bed when I get out; playing with the toy and getting yourself ready for me."

Within forty-five minutes, Jordan and I were both showered and prepped. I walked from the bathroom, my cock throbbing and begging for what we both knew was coming next. I found Jordan in the middle of the bed, his eyes watching me intently as his lube-slick fingers stretched his hole.

"Wanted to wait for you before I did anything more," he said gruffly.

I crawled onto the bed and reached for the silicone toy. "I'm here now. Wanna watch." I knew he'd used the toy before, but I loved that he was waiting on me to see him for the first time.

Jordan smeared the head of the dildo with lube and pressed it against his entrance. He groaned soft and low as his body opened to the invasion. I stroked my cock as I watched his pucker stretch around the toy.

"Fuck," I muttered as Jordan slid the silicone in and out. I took hold of the dildo and fucked him with it for a few moments.

"Stop, want you. Need you," Jordan panted.

Not needing to be told twice, I tossed the toy to the side and slicked my shaft. "How do you want it?"

Jordan spread his legs, his knees falling wide open. "Like this. Wanna watch you. Wanna see your face when your cock takes my virgin hole."

I groaned. "Fuck. You're killing me."

He smiled up at me seductively. "Don't die yet. I need that cock first."

Without waiting another moment, I pressed the leaking head of my dick against his hole and slowly pushed inside. I hissed as Jordan's tight heat pulled me deeper and when my balls met his warm skin, I paused to catch my breath. "You good?"

Jordan's legs wrapped around my waist and he took my hand to pull me close. When our chests met, he cupped a hand around my neck and kissed me slow and deep. "I'm good. Feel so fuckin' full. Wanna feel you come in me."

"That's the plan," I dipped my tongue between his lips

and began to rock my hips. I'd topped a few guys in my time —even though I gravitated toward bottoming—but none of them had ever made me feel the way Jordan did. Skin-to-skin, sweaty heat, soft caresses, whispered words, and knowing I was the only man who had ever been inside his body made our lovemaking all the more special.

A cacophony of slapping skin, long, low moans, and satisfying grunts filled the air as I continued to thrust deep into Jordan's ass, my balls already threatening to blow.

"Wanna come with you," I whispered. "Stroke yourself." I propped up on my hands to watch as Jordan took his thick cock in his hand and began to pump.

"Oh fuck," he groaned. "Not gonna last if you keep hitting that spot."

"Then I'm doing it right," I teased as I brushed a kiss over his lips and continued to thrust my hips as he jacked his cock.

Our pace and breathing increased, the sounds of our sex growing louder with each second, and I finally couldn't hold back any longer. My cock exploded in Jordan's ass with pulse after pulse as I shot my hot release.

Jordan's ass clenched and he moaned. "Fuck, that's so good." He caught my chin and kissed me. "Ride me and let me fill your ass," he growled.

I pulled gently from Jordan's ass and shifted to straddle his torso. Reaching behind, I took his rock-hard shaft in hand and directed it to my greedy hole. My body opened for his cock and I moaned as his thickness filled me. I began to rock my hips. "Fuck me. Come in me."

Jordan took hold of my hips and thrust up over and over. Within moments, he let loose a long, low groan and spilled his hot cum deep in my ass as my body clenched around him.

"Holy shit," I mumbled as I shifted forward and pressed a

kiss against his lips. "I love you so damn much. That was fucking amazing."

Jordan's spent cock slipped from my body and he rolled us to our sides. "I love you. Even if stolen weekends are all we get, I'll never want anything but a life with you. However we can get it."

My heart soared and my mind was immediately made up.

I ROLLED from Jordan's arms and checked the text that had buzzed me awake.

"Everything okay?" Jordan asked, pressing his front to my back with a kiss to my shoulder.

I sighed. "Yeah, Gramps is heading back to the city. Wanted me to know he was leaving early."

"Stay," Jordan whispered. "I'll take you home tonight after we finish chores."

"Nah, that won't work." I tried to keep a straight face.

"Why? We can spend all day together and I'll take you home tonight. Or tomorrow even."

"Don't need a ride." I tossed my phone onto the side table and rolled to face Jordan.

He raised a brow. "You don't?"

I shook my head. "I don't need a ride *home* because I'm already home. My home is with you; wherever you are, my heart is home."

Jordan's eyes searched mine as if trying to figure out the punchline. "Wait, what?"

I smiled. "I'm staying in Kingsley. I wouldn't be so bold as to assume I could just live with you, so maybe you could help me find a place?"

Jordan kissed me, our teeth clanging as he made a noise

that sounded like a laugh and a sob. "Are you fucking kidding me? You're staying? For real?"

"If you'll have me. I can do my job from here. Gramps is moving here permanently and he gave me the idea—kinda gave me the permission I needed I guess."

"Of course, I'll have you," Jordan whispered and cupped my face. "You don't *have* to, if you want your own place, but I want you here."

"I want to be here." My eyes stung. "I just didn't want to assume."

"No, it's perfect." He kissed me again. "Holy fuck, I can't believe this is happening."

"Believe it. We're the epitome of a happy ending for city boy meets country boy." I kissed him with a huge smile, my heart nearly bursting.

Jordan touched my face, his eyes wet and wide. "This is real?"

Hank chose that moment to crow as if his damn life depended on it.

I chuckled. "If I'm willing to put up with that damn rooster, you better believe it's real. If I have anything to say about it, it's forever." I brushed kisses over his tear-stained cheeks.

"Forever," he whispered. "Welcome home, Oxford."

EPILOGUE

JORDAN

FALL. Two years later.

I couldn't take my eyes off Marc.

We stood in the colorful backyard of Ellie's BnB, hand-in-hand, as the minister spoke of love and commitment. Our wedding consisted only of family and a couple of friends. Marc's sister, Marissa, and her family were there. Marcus Kingsley, Sr. had been invited but didn't return the RSVP. My sister, her husband, and their kids came to the farm for the event. Ms. Bethany and Scott were there. And of course, Ellie and Ed.

Our babies—as Marc liked to call the two dogs we'd adopted as puppies over a year ago—were happily sitting at our feet as if they understood the day was special. The big oafs would be frolicking around later and begging treats from anyone they thought would give them something.

The dogs were brothers and the day we'd picked them up from the Shilesville animal shelter, the girl at the front desk had brought them out and given Marc a flirty smile as she'd handed the puppies over. "Here they are, Marc's brothers," she'd cooed.

We'd laughed all the way home about the comment.

"So, what are we going to name them?" I'd wondered as we unloaded the puppies at the farm. "They can't just be Marc's brothers."

"Wait," Marc had said. "That's perfect. Marc's brothers? As in Marx brothers? What were their names?" He'd pulled out his phone and searched for the Marx brothers. "That's it. Harpo and Zeppo."

"What about Groucho?" I'd teased.

"Nah, our babies aren't grouchy. I like these names. Harpo and Zeppo. Harp and Zepp. Perfect."

So, just like the brothers in real life, the blond lab puppy had become Harpo and the chocolate lab had become Zeppo. They were the most spoiled dogs in the history of dogs, but they were also super smart and well-behaved. Marc and I had talked about possibly having children one day, but for the time being, Harpo and Zeppo were the only babies we needed.

Marc's transition to Kingsley and us living together had gone as smooth as butter. Surprisingly, my *coming out* hadn't been painful at all. Ms. Bethany and Scott likely had a lot to do with that. Both had been very kind and accepting when I'd told them Marc would be living with me—as my partner. Word seemed to travel around town pretty quickly, but my egg and veggie sales never took a hit. My carpentry business was lucrative beyond my wildest dreams. And Marc and I were free to be ourselves in town; not a single person had given us a problem. Maybe because the ones who didn't like it were just keeping their mouths shut. Maybe because of the Kingsley name and my history with the town as well. Whatever the reason, everything had gone better than we could have imagined.

One year into telecommuting to Kingsley Sales and Logistics, Marc admitted that he wasn't in love with the job any longer. He sold his shares to Marissa and basically told Marcus, Sr. to kiss his ass. Ed had smiled proudly the whole time.

Marc opened his own online consulting business. His company is super successful and Marc is beyond happy.

We both are.

"I understand you gentlemen had a few words you wanted to say?" the minister asked.

I swallowed thickly and gave Marc's hand a squeeze. "I'd accepted that I couldn't have a love life *and* my farm. I was fine with that. And then you came along. You made me realize what I was missing. You made me want more." I slid a solid tungsten ring onto his finger—country boys need rings that can withstand hard work. "I promise to love you for the rest of our lives. I promise to stand by your side, help you through the rough times, and to never *ever* make my recovering city boy camp on the dirty ground."

Marc's laughter bubbled through smiling lips as he wiped his eyes and pulled a matching ring from his pocket. "Jordan," he began, but the low rumble and shrill whistle of an approaching train filled the air. He glanced in the direction of the train and huffed with a roll of his eyes. "If it wasn't going to be Hank, I should have known that damn train would interrupt."

The minister smiled. "The joys of country living."

We paused as the train went by, the dogs howling to match the whistle.

"Well, after that rudeness," Marc started, "let me start again. Jordan, I thought coming to this place was the worst punishment that could ever happen to me. When I met you, I thought we could have fun for a short time. But in that short time, you taught me how to slow down. You taught me to appreciate the simple things in life. You taught me to look deep inside and to see the real me." He slid the ring on my finger. "You're my forever. I promise to stand with you, make a home with you, and support you in whatever ways you need. I love you more than bread and gravy or corn on the cob." He chuckled and I couldn't help the teary laughter that escaped me. "I promise to feed you sushi, take you to musicals, and give you my sweet tea every single time."

The minister pronounced us husbands. I pulled Marc close and kissed him as our friends and family cheered and the Marx brothers barked happily.

Later, we ate the best of downhome food, made toasts, savored wedding cake, and danced together as husbands and with our family and friends. As our field party reception continued late into the night, Marc pulled me to the far side of the barn.

"What's wrong?" I asked between feverish kisses.

"Not a thing. But I have a request for my husband."

"Anything," I answered with a smile before kissing him again as our hips rocked together.

"Take me home," he whispered.

And that's exactly what I did.

THE END

ALSO BY A.D. ELLIS

Let Love In M/M age-gap, forced proximity, dad's best friend, bisexual-awakening romance

Let Love Win M/M brother's best friend romance

Buried Secrets Romantic suspense stand-alone title. Coming soon to AUDIO!

Silver in the City (3 books- meet the Silver crew you read about in Forged in the City) Available on AUDIO!

Forged in the City (3 books- a spin-off series from Silver in the City) Available on AUDIO

The BJ Boys Series (3 books, small town, big love) Available on AUDIO

Forever Better Together (friends to lovers) Coming soon to AUDIO!

His Reluctant Cowboy (age gap, opposites attract, cowboy romance) Available on AUDIO!

What Blooms Beneath (LGBT Fantasy romance) Available on AUDIO!

Sawyer

(this was the first M/M I wrote and you may remember Sawyer and Luke being mentioned in Barrett & Ivan as well as in Ryker & Gavin)

Start Something About Him with a **FREE** short story:

(The Beginning https://instafreebie.com/free/84Cxr)

Then continue with the other stand-alone titles in the series (available to read FREE for Kindle Unlimited subscribers):

Bryan & Jase

Brody & Nick

Barrett & Ivan

Braeton & Drew

Ryker & Gavin

Kade & Cameron

Or grab the boxset HERE.

Plus several other titles:

Devoted (a Something About Him novella)

Saving Us

Stranded Hearts (a short story)

Eli & Gage (a Something About Him short story)

Escape (a 3-book collection of fun stories)

A.D.'s first stories (all male/female except Sawyer which is male/male) are in the Torey Hope and Torey Hope: The Later Years series. Find the 8 book box set HERE or you can find each individual title on Amazon.

For Nicky

Because of Beckett

Christmas in Torey Hope

Loving Josie

Decker

Sawyer

Zach

Kendrick

ACKNOWLEDGMENTS

It's always so hard to write this part because I'm worried I'll forget someone without meaning to.

Readers- you are the reason I write. As long as you continue reading my stories, I'll continue writing them. Thank you for your support.

Bloggers- your support, reviews, and promotion are very much appreciated. Thank you!

My author buddies- I don't know that I could keep doing this without our brainstorm sessions, laughter, road trips, meals, wine, and friendship as my support.

Thank you to my alpha readers, betas, editors, proofreaders, and ARC readers! Your eyes and input are beyond important to me.

Brett and Gage- as usual, I doubt you even grasp how much your support, input, and friendship mean to me. This author journey has brought many wonderful things into my life, and you both are two of the BEST! I'm blessed to call you friends.

My family and friends- thank you for your love and support, always.

ABOUT THE AUTHOR

A.D. Ellis is an Indiana girl, born and raised. She spends much of her time in central Indiana as an instructional coach/teacher in the inner city of Indianapolis, being a mom to two amazing school-aged children, and wondering how she and her husband of almost two decades have managed to not drive each other insane. A lot of her time is also devoted to phone call avoidance and her hatred of cooking.

She loves chocolate, wine, pizza, and naps along with reading and writing romance. These loves don't leave much time for housework, much to the chagrin of her husband. Who would pick cleaning the house over a nap or a good book? She uses any extra time to increase her fluency in sarcasm.

Find all of Ellis' contemporary romance and male/male romance at www.adellisauthor.com

FREE books-- sign up at bit.ly/ADEllisNews for a FREE male/female romance.

Sign up at http://www.subscribepage.com/ADEllisNewsMMRomance for a FREE male/male romance book.

www.ingramcontent.com/pod-product-compliance
Lightning Source LLC
Chambersburg PA
CBHW030113030726
47498CB00007B/2364